A COVENANT OF ICE

Also by Karin Lowachee

The Crowns of Ishia
The Mountain Crown
The Desert Talon

The Warchild Mosaic
Warchild
Burndive
Cagebird

The Middle Light Trilogy
The Gaslight Dogs

A COVENANT OF ICE

KARIN LOWACHEE

SOLARIS

First published 2025 by Solaris
an imprint of Rebellion Publishing Ltd,
Riverside House, Osney Mead,
Oxford, OX2 0ES, UK

www.solarisbooks.com

ISBN: 978-1-83786-513-0

Copyright © 2025 Karin Lowachee

The right of the author to be identified as the author
of this work has been asserted in accordance with the
Copyright, Designs and Patents Act 1988.

All rights reserved. No part of this publication may be
reproduced, stored in a retrieval system, or transmitted,
in any form or by any means, electronic, mechanical,
photocopying, recording or otherwise, without the prior
permission of the copyright owners.

This book is a work of fiction. Names, characters, places
and incidents are products of the author's imagination or
are used fictitiously.

10 9 8 7 6 5 4 3 2 1

A CIP catalogue record for this book is available from
the British Library.

Designed & typeset by Rebellion Publishing

Printed in Denmark

For Johann

In loving memory
forever in the light of the aurora

LILLEY MARKED TIME now by magnitudes of madness. Maybe it had always been so, since his earliest memories of the villa in Diam where his family were slaves. Only now the insanity was doubled by the presence of the dragon. In dreams, in his waking hours, the dragon, the dragon. He became a stranger to sleep. He was becoming a stranger to the finer elements of emotion, as if this folly with the dragon Raka and the man Raka was wrapped up in one churning chaos in his body. This chaos was shearing away the sharpness that had been forged through thirty-two years of life in war and servitude.

Now he moved through the days like a dumb blunt object and more than once his beloved Janan had to nudge him into some semblance of pointed attention. "Na, I'm here," Lilley would tell him, with a smile, but neither of them were convinced. The lie had become so pervasive that Janan no longer called him on it, just watched him with ever-increasing concern. They'd fallen into a routine of helplessness. Janan couldn't parse his chaos even if sometimes he felt it through their bond, and Méka couldn't see through it to sense, not even the Greatmothers could, so she told him to write everything down as if that could separate his coherence from confusion. What he was feeling, what he saw, both in dream and waking. But fashioning words for things made for scary shapes. A year since they'd left Kattaka in the north, a year since he'd found Janan again after half a decade of separation, and he now possessed a book of frightening ciphers. Flipping back through the papers in his hide-bound journal, the scratch of ink resembled the ravings of a madman. Maybe it was time he accepted the diagnosis.

Despite Raka's harassment at all hours, Lilley still held to one phantomless dream and he shared it often with Janan like it was a thread that must be woven back and forth between them or else he'd unravel. It was a dream they knew well because they'd spun it back in their fighting days when such musings were part of the armor to keep the madness of war at bay. It had worked, for the most part.

We'll go south, Lilley would start. Whether they were around a campfire or on their backs looking up at the shadowed ceiling of their tent, shivering through winters or sweating through some months of sun. And Janan would carry the thought forward with, *We'll find a place that doesn't yet exist to anyone else*. Lilley would continue, *So there would be no more fighting*. Janan would counter, *But there would be a beach. White crystal sand like snow. Sirra Kusa*, they called it. After a name they'd discovered in a mapbook given to Janan by an old Mazoön warrior long ago. It went on, their elaborate fantasy of freedom.

They'd come south, in the end, if separately. Not to a beach and not to a place that didn't also know war. Mazemoor was who they'd once warred *with*. The Mazoön called them refugees. It was another magnitude of his madness, that he could travel the limited paths of this land with the scattered Ba'Suon families and his impossible dragon, and think himself free.

Now in his dreams, instead of beaches, all Lilley saw was snow. And the cold of winter followed him into his waking hours.

LATELY, HE COULDN'T recall a scene of himself and Janan without some accompanying interruptive memory of Raka. True, Raka had spent the latter years of the war in their company, all of them under Lord Shearoji's command, but trying to keep his present alive with warm thoughts of his beloved were undermined by the appearance of the Ba'Suon man, who he now called traitor. Those were some of the final feelings he'd felt for Raka, even if in the end he'd tried to lure him back to the living.

The last moments locked in Raka's stare as Fortune City collapsed in flames. Years of camaraderie and one act of betrayal crashed into the center of his chest and stole his breath. Yet knowing in that moment that Raka was about to give himself up to the stars formed a fist of desperation around his heart. *I can't lose you and Janan both*. Maybe it had been that last thought that had instigated his chaos. An invitation that punched through all the anger and spite. He'd been trying to breathe ever since, wracked by a complicated guilt.

The first snowfall at Fort Nemiha had heralded Raka's appearance in their lives five years into their war. He and Janan built a fire outside their tent and watched the embers fly up to the dark sky and meld with the crystal flakes and the cat eyes of the starry night. Beyond the tall timber pillars of the fort's walls, the ocean exhaled in regular waves, pushing a chill through the troop. Tourmaline had launched for her nocturnal hunt at dusk and new recruits walked through the gates in full dark, ushered by flurries. They all watched the ragged procession pass by their tents and line up on the parade ground. Sergeant Yo-han delivered his memorized speech meant to both frighten and embolden the fresh fodder, then the recruits were turned out to find some place to bed down with the regulars. Many wandered around like lost children before clumping together at any offer of warmth. Raka came accompanied by Lord General Shearoji himself, who stood the lad before Lilley and Janan and needlessly pointed out Raka's Ba'Suon nature. "Orient him," was the command, which immediately set him apart from all the other new faces.

Lilley felt how silent and still Janan grew beside him, as if some great hand had decided to turn a key and dim his light of fuel. His harwan's hand shifted to rest on the hilt of one of his blades, which told Lilley that this was nobody Janan cared to call brother. Lilley blew smoke out the side of his mouth and looked this Raka up and down. He couldn't find a single detail of threat on the man. The dark eyes aimed somewhere in front of the fire like he was too cowed to even greet the flames. His hat sat a little lopsided and his woolen coat had seen better weather for certain. Kattakan clothes, not Ba'Suon skins.

"You special or somethin?"

"No."

"Then what's got Shearoji hot and bothered about you?"

Raka shrugged.

"You can sit over there," said Janan, nodding to a log some distance from their fire.

"It's a bitter night," Lilley said, to ameliorate the discussion. He gestured to the seat closer up and across from them. "That'll do. Where you comin from?"

"Here," said Raka, drawing his arms in against his body.

"You're not from here," Janan said.

Lilley noted the aim of their gazes, and if they'd contained bullets at least one of them would be dead. He touched Janan's leg.

"It's too cold to quarrel."

It turned out it was too cold to converse as well, so they sat in warm but not welcome silence until he and Janan retreated to their tent, leaving Raka outside to find his own form of comfort.

A Covenant of Ice

"Why don't you trust him?" Lilley asked his harwan. They created a nimbus of heat around their entwined bodies. His voice fell only as far as the inch of space between their mouths.

Janan touched the side of his face like the shadows were words, and didn't answer immediately. Lamplight reflected in the depths of his eyes, whole histories Lilley knew he'd only started to learn. Janan had tried to explain to him how the Ba'Suon navigated the world but all such descriptions sounded to his understanding like both paradise and torture. To be so knowing of nature as to hear its thoughts, yet feeling then when nature cried out. After every battle with the Mazoön, his harwan often retreated with Tourmaline into apartness and he'd learned not to interrupt. Sometimes he reckoned he'd become a strange anchor to the living for Janan, to life, when so much of their daily enterprise involved the prospect and procreation of death. And so they survived together.

"I don't feel anything from him," Janan said finally.

"He does seem like a closed off fellar."

"No. I mean there's nothing of nature that resides in him. Even Kattakans, even you and your people can resound with a sense of hollowness, and when you're emotional enough it comes to me like the voice of the wind. But there's nothing in him, not even an echo."

"But he's Ba'Suon?"

"So he claims."

"You should ask him which family."

Janan shook his head slowly. "He's not from any family I've ever known."

What other families could exist? The island was not so large that generations of Ba'Suon did not all meet in some fashion in the past. But he didn't get to ask it; his harwan rolled over to face the tent wall and Lilley draped an arm over his ribs.

"Just be careful," Janan said. Quietly, to the shadows.

If only they'd kept to this caution.

AT NIGHT RAKA the dragon liked to splash in the lake. This was not a gentle affair. Lilley heard the beast from inside the mata he shared with Janan and it pricked enough holes in his sleep that consciousness bled through and drowned him. So he grabbed his shirt and trousers and stomped down to the pebbled shore, pulling on his clothes in stutters, as the one hand he had available quickly grew chilled. Late autumn air coursed icy fingers through his hair and down his back. The camp was still dark and silent beyond the night, too early even for the most eager wrangler to be up and about tending to the animals and the communal cooking fire. The eastern horizon behind the Antler Mountains showed not a sliver of red or gold. Dark all the way to the depths, spattered by distant stars. The moon glowed sullenly above. He met its mood as he stood on the shore and watched the diamondback wallop his wings on the surface of the water. It sounded like whale fins and tossed up tsunamis of spray.

A Covenant of Ice

"Can't ya go hunt like the rest of em in the crown?"

Janan's dragon Tourmaline and Méka's dragon Rainfall, both northern queens that he'd named, had taken the smaller southern ones on a night foray, as was their habit. Also among them were a couple younger northern kings, recently gathered in the past five years. The camp's crown numbered only twelve, as many of the Ba'Suon who'd fled south during or after the war had never gathered a dragon. Some had lost them to the war, like Janan's Sephihalé sister Prita. Rainfall, like her rider, was not a combative sort, and Tourmaline was the battle dragon amongst the crown; nobody disputed her. But then there was Raka, the diamondback king who bellowed and bullied his way through the days and nights, and only once in a spell did he listen when Lilley tried to direct him to common sense.

Tonight was not one of those times. The dragon pointedly turned his back on Lilley and slapped his tail on the water. Spray hit Lilley in the face. He sighed and sat, swiping his cheek against his shoulder, and tried to employ the tactic both Janan and Méka encouraged him to practice: be still and breathe. In this state, allegedly, he would be able to better feel Raka's disposition, and clumsy words would not be needed. Raka would send him a combination of images and emotion that was the preferred language of dragons and so encourage the bond.

If the dragon had any inclination to communicate this way with any consistency, the man Raka who was somehow embodied in the creature tended to blockade any such path. Lilley sensed that it was a form of punishment, as if the fact of Raka occupying him *and* the diamondback in this mad manner wasn't punishment enough. So even in some manifestation of death, the Ba'Suon man was a selfish, contrary prick.

For a year he endured the agitation in his body, as if his own skin no longer properly adhered to his muscle and bone. Impulses he grew to doubt seemed to dictate his daily routines; a temper he ordinarily kept under control flared at unpredictable points. The dragon seemed to resonate these moods and amplify them in his own massive body, or maybe sometimes Raka was the source. After a while Lilley could no longer discern the true origin. But he didn't 'hear' the dragon's thoughts like Janan or Méka did, only felt the specific shape of the creature's power and resolve. He couldn't truly parse the man in the midst of it all. Raka, his former companion, seemed to exist in the vagaries of emotion.

Maybe his own frustration now traveled out with enough force to provoke a reaction. The dragon swung his long neck back toward the shore and blinked at Lilley with glowing golden eyes. The creature chuffed. Lilley watched him, still not quite used to the scrutiny of such an unaccustomed force, but unable to look away. Proximity demanded a certain stubborn confrontation, though he harbored no delusion of who was dominant. The dragon likely felt that too. A moment of peace passed between them, then the

A Covenant of Ice

dragon turned his colossal body and splashed slowly to the stretch of rocks and grass on which Lilley waited. Water cascaded off the black scales of his back and dripped from the hollows. Made clean so in his next flight the wind would howl through those scales, creating a song of thunder.

Lilley looked up past the inky shadows cast by the whale-length of the dragon's frame and his fanned wings. The white belly seemed to capture the moonlight. This creature of bones and abyss. "You know you woke me, so what do you want?"

The dragon roared. It cut like a scythe through the camp and the far reaches of the valley, echoing from peak to peak. Lilley covered his ears in the buffet of sound.

Somehow, through the depths of such a racket, he heard a deadened voice, the murmur of a ghost that seemed to be standing against the back of his left shoulder, speaking straight into his ear.

Riders coming to the camp.

ONCE RAKA BEGAN to speak, back in their warring days, something about his minimum openness seemed to crack the initial ice Janan felt toward him. Lilley watched his harwan invite Raka to eat meals with them around their fire, and guide him in their first foray to guard a coastal town against a Mazoön reconnaissance party. When Lilley asked Janan what had changed his mind, his harwan said only that Raka was born from a family that had endured a tragedy and perhaps his first impression had been unkind. "He needs family and I reckon we're it. Besides, Shearoji said to show him the ropes. He's skilled."

And by that Janan meant with the dragons. Tourmaline remained standoffish, but she was rarely amenable to anyone but them. The other dragons in the camp, gathered by the handful of Ba'Suon soldiers in their ranks, took to Raka readily enough. Maybe because he was often found tending to them: washing their scales or grooming their wings.

"There's still something strange about him," said Janan, "but I don't think he's much of a threat. He just hasn't been around many Ba'Suon until now."

"The dragons might like em but your people not so much. Even I can see that."

"We can be kind to him," Janan said.

His first conversation alone with Raka began as they stood guard on the rampart facing the inland road, from where messengers often rode. His eyesight was shit compared to the Ba'Suon man, so it was usually Raka doing the looking while he leaned there and smoked his cigarette, enjoying the stars.

"This land could be beautiful if it weren't for us," he mused.

"You mean you Kattakans? I agree."

Already he found it difficult to tell if Raka was teasing him or not. "We ain't all bad."

"The only good thing about you is the fact Janan tolerates you."

A Covenant of Ice

"He does more than that and I reckon you hear it from your tent next door." He cackled to catch Raka blushing, evident even in the dim light. And so began the tenor of their dynamic. The more he persecuted the other man, the more they seemed to get along.

"Where's your family?" Raka asked.

"You seen em. That tall Ba'Suon and his golden dragon."

"Your born family."

He looked through his smoke at the other man. "That story ain't for early talk. I reckon all the family any of us got goin is here inside these walls."

A strange shadow seemed to course like fingers over Raka's features. "But you'll tell me one day?"

"If it'll make you shut up about it, maybe."

That seemed to appease the peculiar Ba'Suon. "Riders coming," Raka said, and reached for the torch beside them to signal the guards below at the gate.

In the nest pen across the fort, the dragons set up a ruckus of warning.

THE DISTURBANCE FROM the diamondback drew Janan to his side. Other Ba'Suon emerged from various family matas to take a peek. The king dragon's uproar wasn't an unusual event, so most of the people retreated back inside and shut their wooden doors for what protection that would offer against the noise. He still felt even after a year that he ought to apologize for the dragon's ill-timed acting up, but it wasn't like he owned the creature, nor could he tell Raka to leave. The king did what he wanted and they all suffered his whims.

Janan didn't ask why he was out here, and barely glanced at the looming presence of the dragon, who by now had turned to stare toward the south. Instead, Lilley rose to his feet and met his harwan's stare, shivering. Janan stepped toe to toe with him and wrapped his arms around him to offer warmth.

"He spoke to me," Lilley mumbled, mouth pressed to the familiar scent of earth and pine that was soaked into Janan's shirt.

The rubbing palm along his back ceased its attempt to soothe. "What do you mean?"

"I heard words. Specific words. Not a feelin or an image." It wasn't only the cold that made him tremble. He'd never much believed in spirits of any sort, but the hollow voice against his ear had possessed the sense of one, and this telegraphed an unwanted new development to his chaos.

Janan set him back by the shoulders only so they could look at each other directly. "From the suon?"

"From Raka." It was the same, man and dragon, but this concept continued to elude them in concrete ways. "Abhvihin ele Raka's voice."

A significant silence, but his harwan wasn't a man to easily panic. "What did he say?"

"We're gonna get visitors." Saying the words seemed to conjure a confirmation. Across his vision bled a picture of two people upon tall dark horses, cloaked in Mazoön patterns. The Antler Mountains rose up

A Covenant of Ice

on either side of their path, but as the colors drifted one into another, the riders faded completely until all the world became white and he was standing amidst a vista of snow in every direction.

We'll go home. I've waited so long to take you.

"Lilley."

He blinked back the white and Janan now clutched his arms as if to shake him.

"I'm here, I'm here."

"You weren't."

"Ain't nothin new. Just another shade of it." He thought of smiling like it was a game of dice he could throw, but the inclination died in his palm. He was getting colder the longer they stood there. He'd been growing colder for a year and no amount of body heat or fires could chase it away.

"Was he speaking to you again?" His harwan touched his cheek. "Abhvihin ele Raka?"

"A little."

"What more?"

He looked over Janan's shoulder and shook his head, reluctant to say the words aloud lest they bring to life more strange scenery. Méka emerged from the dark, taking both their attention. Naturally she'd heard the diamondback too, only she wasn't as put off about his mercurial behavior as the rest of the camp. Even in the blurred night, her expression showed worry.

"What's he doing?" She meant the dragon.

Lilley looked at the king sitting with his back to them. Wings folded in, tail in a flat curl along the ground. He didn't move, only the sound of hot gusts of breath from deep in his chest gave evidence of his vitality. Otherwise, he could have been some ancient monument carved from obsidian and alabaster and gold.

"He's waiting," Lilley said. And he knew then, all at once, that this waiting had started a year ago in Eastern Kattaka, perhaps longer, in the country that had once been an island of Ishia where the Ba'Suon had thrived. There, Abhvihin ele Raka had given up his life in Fortune City, raging fire and death upon all who stood in his way. They'd thought Raka had returned to the cosmos, but months of this chaos and what plagued Lilley in madness was just another manifestation of being.

Like a spoken curse laid upon the living.

LILLEY POSSESSED HIS mother Clarra's temper, the kind that ran ice cold like it was born from the deep aquifers below the sunning surface of the earth. It was the first magnitude of his madness that only one person, his harwan Janan, had ever truly felt. Most of the time he'd learned to disguise that bloodswell with smiles and sharp words, otherwise the world could exhaust him with its insanity. He never had much of a problem killing; it was everything after that which rubbed against the insides of his ribcage.

Clarra dreamed of the south too, an escape from the toil at the hands of their masters. He remembered the consequence of such dreams as if he'd written it down

A Covenant of Ice

in decisive detail. The way his old masters stood her against the ivy wall of their villa and shot her through the front of her skull.

She'd tried too many times to run away. She dared to take him with her, once, her only child. Under Kattakan law, that was considered theft of the masters' property. His father had begged for Lilley's life, citing age as a reason for forgiveness. "The boy's old enough to agree to the escape," claimed their masters. Eight years old.

He remembered looking those men in the eyes and knew they marked his wrath. But in the end he was too valuable to punish. He had able hands and some show of fearful acquiescence, they thought. He'd learned there were magnitudes of fear too. At sixteen years old he enlisted for his freedom, a mandate by the Kattakan government to encourage a stable of soldiers. The war became his new master and he never saw his father again. He fought the wrong enemy on the back of a queen dragon. He fell in love.

He should've turned Tourmaline and his Ba'Suon harwan, with all that cousin rage, upon the city of Diam. This wasn't quite a dream that he shared with Janan, but more of an illicit wish. They spoke of it like people did when they were fixing to make sense of the world, or at least to vindicate it. The precision of their fantasy took on a cartographer's skill. He knew they formed words for their vengeance because they would never enact it, not the least reason being such mass death was anathema to any Ba'Suon and Janan bore the brunt of that experience already by merely riding into battle. Yet the taboo of vengeance became a comfort to fulfill even in phantasm. The obverse image of their white sand beach.

Then we wouldn't have to go south, he'd say to Janan. *We could find a piece of land right here, in the paths of your ancestors. In the dreams of mine.* The bloodline of his people going back generations, who'd fled their Kattakan overseers on the mainland.

And they would all be free.

HE AND HIS companions stood at the edge of the quiet camp. Pink light stretched across the valley as the sun barely opened its broad eyelid. A dozen young handlers went about their daybreak chores, feeding the goats and horses and chickens. Tourmaline and Rainfall had returned with the crown, and now the queens loomed behind him, Méka, and Janan. Gold and gray. Raka had taken to the sky, scouring the pastel clouds. Lilley told his companions that the riders would be coming from the south. They guessed it would be from Tallo, the closest Mazoön town.

Méka hadn't reacted much to the revelation that Raka had spoken to him. What was one more peculiarity?

"Maybe this way you can tell him to leave you alone." The woman demonstrated a hidden humor, but he knew she bore a heavy regret over the fact she hadn't been able to help the man when he'd been corporeally alive. They spoke of it sometimes when they were alone—out on a hunt or sitting by some body of water wherever their people had made camp in the seasonal paths of their going. Janan had less tolerance for such conversation, even if Lilley knew some latent regret existed there too. He couldn't blame Janan for blockading any kind conclusion to their history with the dead man. Janan had known Raka too well.

Sometimes, Lilley wondered if his harwan saw Raka when they looked at each other, and if that was some of the reason for the growing silence between them. Sometimes he'd reach for Janan's hand and squeeze it bloodless, no words, and would only release him once he felt it back. Their lovemaking took on a sheen of desperation, but he quelled that oftentimes by closeness afterward. In spent exhaustion the careful barriers came down; he felt their bond fully and they were whole, just the two of them.

Now, standing at the edge of the camp, most of what he felt was Raka, the man and the dragon. He knew where precisely the dragon was in the sky without having to look, and something of the man breathed in the back corner of his mind. Waiting.

Can't you leave me be? He tried Méka's suggestion but was only met with silence.

They all were dressed in full Ba'Suon kit, Méka and Janan with their blades and he with his holstered pistol. The dragon scales on their clothing captured the growing morning light with hints of gold. Though it would be foolish to approach with hostile intent on a camp of three adult northern dragons, they couldn't dismiss the possibility entirely. People were known for foolish acts of arrogance, and it didn't matter on which island they stood.

The advancing horses didn't falter or fret, despite Raka's shadowed, thundering pass overhead as soon as the riders emerged into view. Two, as foretold. So these were no ordinary travelers, nor were they riding ordinary horses. Government, he thought, right before Méka called out the details of the riders' attire. The broad black hats and Mazoön leaf-shape patterns on wide-sleeved tunics, one blue, one green. Her Ba'Suon vision was some telescopic wonder he had yet to fully understand. Janan had the same.

"I know her." His harwan moved forward to meet the horses, eyes fixed on the approaching figures. "An agent of Internal Security. Phinia Dellerm'el. I don't recognize the other one."

"He's Ba'Suon," said Méka, a certain flat caution in her voice.

Lilley looked at both his companions but other than their recognition, they kept their resolve contained, hands away from their blades. He set his palm lightly on the grip of his gun but didn't shift from his easy stance. No sense leading with provocation, even if Dellerm'el was the woman who'd compelled Janan to work as some sort of personal gun on behalf of the Mazoön government. He knew very little about that time, and not for want of asking. His harwan wasn't inclined to go into detail, which only told Lilley

A Covenant of Ice

those years had inflicted the kind of suffering Janan had endured in the war, a Ba'Suon charged to harm another part of living nature, even people.

So this Agent Dellerm'el came with yet another Ba'Suon on her right hand. If this one was similarly compelled, he wouldn't be surprised.

The black horses trotted the final few feet before stopping close enough for Janan to take hold of the bridle cheek strap of the agent's mount. Phinia Dellerm'el swung her leg over the neck of her ride and jumped down to the ground. Her young Ba'Suon companion remained ahorse. He couldn't have been more than a twig, barely out of adolescence. Wide tanned cheekbones peppered with faint freckles and blinkless, pale amber eyes. Something about that stare made Lilley's skin crawl, as the kid's gaze fixed on him and refused to move. He didn't move either and the discomfort spread. It worked an irritation in his chest. The licorice in his mouth turned stale and he spat it to the ground. The Ba'Suon boy still didn't blink.

Overhead, Raka bellowed. A feeling of warning seemed to slant from the clouds like rain and Lilley resisted the urge to swipe his forearm across his face as the dragon's suspicion ran in rivulets down his skin. The agent cast a nervous glance to the clouds then looked back at them, while Raka flung through the sky with restless attention, his shadow coursing back and forth.

The Ba'Suon boy didn't shift his stare.

Janan stepped in front of Lilley and blocked the

view. Tourmaline fanned her wings back in a display of dominance and tilted her face to glare at Dellerm'el with her unscarred eye. Likely she recognized the agent. A brief impression of a desert heat spread along Lilley's back. Rainfall, as usual, sat composed, but her alertness was another kind of threat if this agent had any knowledge of dragon behavior.

"Sephihalé ele Janan." A perfunctory nod from Dellerm'el. Then her dark eyes beneath the brim of her hat found Méka and finally him. She lingered there like her young companion. He let her with a meddling stare of his own. "You must be Havinger Lilley, Janan's harwan."

He didn't acknowledge it. To hear the sacred Ba'Suon word out of her mouth felt vaguely like a defilement. Janan lured back her focus with a blunt question. "Why are you here?"

She looked up and all around at the lightening valley. The silhouette of the mountains with their palmate curves. Carefully her eyes avoided the towering dragons, even when Rainfall flicked her satin gray wings and bowed her long head closer. Thin fingers of smoke stretched toward the intruders from the dragon's nostrils. Dellerm'el wasn't a large woman in stature but even in the compact space of her being she evinced a prominent presence. As though a globe of some power granted to her by her government threatened to eclipse all else around her. He'd seen the like in Kattaka, the invulnerability of those who perceived they possessed an unbreakable power.

A Covenant of Ice

She ignored the dragons and spoke only to Janan. "I need to talk to you."

"You talk to us," he said. "And to the Greatmothers."

"No," said the agent. "Your harwan, yes, if you insist. But nobody else. Where?"

Méka spoke for the first time, in a tone that didn't entertain argument. "You'll talk to all three of us." Her stare shifted to the boy. "And who are you?"

The kid still sitting ahorse looked slowly at Méka as if she'd called him out of a daze. "Gherijtana ele Railé."

Something about the name made both Lilley's Ba'Suon companions startle, and only seemed to set the Mazoön agent on edge.

"Somewhere private," she said. "Now."

Despite the fact the agent was as close to an enemy as they had in this country, she was still a guest of Méka's mata, and Dellerm'el at least had enough knowledge of Ba'Suon ways to remove her boots and hat inside the door. She placed them on the bench along the mata's painted wall and sat herself in a contained pose on the woven rug. The kid Railé did the same. His curious presence cast a deep unease through the tent, but whether it was from his name or his current association, or both, Lilley had no time to inquire. A pervasive smoky-sweet scent carried on the lad's clothes even from a distance.

As Méka and Janan moved in the small rituals of

greeting, passing out warmed cloths to wash their faces and hands, Lilley remained standing, leaning his shoulder against one of the mata poles behind the agent. She didn't like it from the way she looked back at him with disapproval etched around her mouth. He stared at her with his handless arm tucked against his ribs and his right hand resting on the grip of his pistol. She turned back to face the Ba'Suon.

"Are you armed?" Janan asked her.

"On my horse. Which I trust will be taken care of."

"They will be," said Méka, who knelt by the low iron stove, making them tea. They waited for this ceremonial welcome to conclude when the Ba'Suon and the Mazoön held warm cups in their hands. He didn't take tea and Méka didn't offer. His hand needed to be free for his gun.

The fresh scent of mint filled the tall space of the mata. Above, through the hand-holes of the mata's wooden frame and canvas roof, the sky showed a delicate blue. Same sky as shone on them in Kattaka. Sometimes he felt no distance from then to now, but then sometimes lately it was difficult to remember that time at all. Even as he stood there, Raka's vision from his flight overhead bled into the present and it took some avid concentration to rid himself of the skein.

"What do you want?" Janan asked the Mazoön agent.

She sipped her tea before answering. "The Kattakans are making forays into the north. The far north."

The news sank into silence. A subtle wing of recognition flit at the corner of his mind. A brief image

A Covenant of Ice

of a shard-white sky and a diamond sun. A crawl of cold inside his collar. Beyond the camp in the staircase of the clouds, Raka wheeled, dragging a deafening silence in his wake. The pressure of it started to pound behind Lilley's eyes in earnest.

Dellerm'el carried on. "As you may assume, we don't want the Kattakans to claim yet another region along this archipelago. We understand there are also dragons there, if no Ba'Suon any longer."

Méka said, "Why are you telling us this? We have no control over the Kattakans, as you well know."

"My government feels that if representatives of Mazemoor were to stake claim to the far north, the Kattakans would have no avenue for incursion."

He wanted to laugh. The Mazoön had fought a ten-year war with his people and this was their conclusion. Janan looked at him as they shared the thought. But it was wiser to let this woman continue to speak.

"We believe they wouldn't incite another conflict if they were met with a Ba'Suon and his battle dragon, wearing the badge of Mazemoor."

"You're too arrogant about my abilities," Janan said.

"We would also send an enastramyth with you to fortify the claim."

"No," said Janan. "I won't deal anymore with your enastramyths."

"Nobody should lay claim to the far north," Méka said. "The suon there are not like the ones you know. From all the accounts of my family and many of the

Karin Lowachee

families of the southern Ba'Suon, only Raka's family Abhvihin could covenant with them. Raka's family no longer exists. I understand Janan told you this."

"He did," said Dellerm'el.

"Your enastramyth," said Janan. "Do you wish to set up a claim in the far north so that you can drain the land like you do your own island? Hasn't enough of Ishia been used by your people?"

Lilley watched the chagrin flitter across the agent's face. So, she had come here thinking she could twist her way into their agreement. The boy Railé said nothing, only looked into his teacup like it could tell him his fortune.

Dellerm'el met Janan's eyes. "Bordering Eastern Kattaka both in the north and south would only strengthen our position against any possible future aggression. You forget they consist of an entire nation across the ocean, the resources of which we are unaware, only that they don't seem to lack for soldiers. How long do you think they'll be satisfied with their single stake in this region?"

They didn't answer her. This attempt to lecture them on the nature of conquest contained that familiar arrogance Janan had pointed out. Nobody knew the nature of conquest better than the Ba'Suon. They lived in the result of it and Mazemoor was only a part of that reality.

Now she seemed impatient at their silence. Finally, Janan said, "Are you commanding us to go or is this truly a request?"

A Covenant of Ice

"I came to *you*, Sephihalé."

"You removed that tether of mythicism from me, supposedly, but it seems to have a long lead."

Anger flashed in her eyes like lightning behind clouds. "You've benefitted from our land. All of you." She gathered herself to her feet and bowed briefly to Méka. "I thank you for the tea, Suonkang ele Mékahalé. I'll return in a week, after you've had some time to discuss my government's proposal amongst your Greatmothers. Hopefully you'll see this expedition will serve all of our people."

Lilley said, "What about him?"

They all looked at Gherijtana ele Railé. The agent said, "He is the enastramyth of which I spoke. He'll remain here in your camp to represent our interests in your council with the Greatmothers."

Lilley didn't need to be Ba'Suon to feel the sudden clamor of caution and alarm that buzzed between his companions.

"You have questions," said the boy, "and I'll answer them."

"Yes," said Méka. "You will." And to the agent: "I'll walk you to your horse." She glanced at Lilley and Janan before pulling on her boots at the door and preceding the agent out of the mata.

Janan remained sitting and Lilley moved to stand just outside of Railé's periphery. The boy glanced up and back at him with that same piercing attention.

"I reckon you can go outside now, son, and keep your southern magic to yourself."

The boy left the mata without argument.

Janan watched him leave and waited for the door to shut. "Don't tell him your name."

"I remember," Lilley said. The urgency of the caution, even before any discussion of the fact this Ba'Suon kid somehow possessed the knowledge of a Mazoön enastramyth, spoke to what little Janan had told him of his time in the desert, working for the Mazoön government. Most of those details were about the nature of their enastramyths and how it was possible to be trapped in their power just from uttering his name to them. "I ain't fixin to make friends, though it's a small wonder why he'd align with them and their knowing."

Janan began to wash out the teacups in a metal basin on the stove. Lilley recognized the need for distraction, to move his hands. "The family Gherijtana are an eccentric lot. One of the oldest families of the Ba'Suon, almost as old as the family Suonkang. Some say they're perpetually in the cosmos."

"What's that mean?"

"They travel the paths of smoke." Janan made a wave motion with his hand. "Constantly. Not just for ceremony or healing. As far as I know, though, none of them came south to Mazemoor. They only went deeper into the land where the Kattakans have yet to fully explore."

"Except for this lad."

"His strangeness goes beyond his family," Janan said quietly, concentrating on the cups. "I sense it like I did Raka."

A Covenant of Ice

Lilley knelt by his harwan and took up a drying cloth. He balanced the washed teacup on his wrist and wiped it clean. "He's the same as Raka?"

"No. But there's something in his presence. Méka must feel it too."

"We'll ask her. Whatever the nature of his power, we'll watch it."

Janan didn't reply. The washing seemed to take his focus more than the task required.

The pressure behind Lilley's eyes dimmed in the roil of his concern. He leaned his shoulder to his harwan's. "Don't worry. If he looks at you wrong I'll make Raka eat him."

Janan laughed. It felt like a concession to the universe that life continued to be absurd. Lilley elbowed him and got elbowed back. For a few moments they engaged in such useless warfare until Janan snatched the cloth from his hand and whipped it against his arm. As the cups were dry and put away, this became their new occupation until Janan successfully harassed him onto his back. He gave up and simply stared at the mata ceiling where Méka had painted a series of circles and diamonds to represent the cosmos. Janan tossed himself down beside him and together they contemplated the constellate image of the night sky.

Silence had never been a barrier between them, not until lately. So he asked this gently, turning his head to look at his harwan's profile: "Will you tell me about your experience with enastramyths?"

Janan didn't meet his stare. "I did."

"Not all of it." When the quiet persisted: "I know about Eben Wisterel and his land. What happened to you and Prita and Omala. But the years after—"

Janan sat up, looking toward the red door of the mata.

Lilley touched his back and remained where he was to negate the alarm and hopefully the discomfort. At least Janan didn't shake off his hand. "You said the Mazoön train their enastramyths in universities. You encountered more than Wisterel when you worked for em. It could help us understand what we might face with this Gherijtana kid."

"All you need to know," said his harwan, glancing back down at him, "is if it comes to it, I'll do to that kid what I did to the rest."

The buzzing in his head went completely silent. And so, it seemed, did the camp outside. All that came to him along the strong twine of their bond was pain. He curled his fingers into Janan's back. "I ain't askin that of you, beloved."

"You didn't have to."

"I don't want you to have to kill anybody ever again. Not even for me."

Janan didn't respond.

Lilley tugged on the back of his shirt. "Do you hear me?"

Sometimes, his harwan's uncharacteristic green eyes could sharpen like sea glass. They cut toward him. "You're the only one I would kill for again."

The mata door creaked open and Méka stood on the threshold. She didn't re-enter. She looked at them

A Covenant of Ice

on the floor and her grave expression was enough to make Lilley sit up. His hand remained on Janan's back, feeling him breathe. It picked up a pace.

"The agent's gone," she said. "Let's talk to the Greatmothers."

Make them listen.

In the sky, the diamondback bellowed again. The dragon was somewhere directly above the mata. Janan and Méka looked up, but he didn't have to. The walls of the mata seemed to exhale and with it the voice pushed against his right ear at the same time the dragon called overhead.

We have to go north.

The circle of the mata spun until all colors and details blurred. The soft texture of Janan's shirt disappeared from under his hand and instead when he clenched his fingers, snow flurry whipped around his fist. He sat on a rocky rise overlooking the white tundra. The sky was sallow like a banner of unbleached canvas and in the distance some deep sound like felled boulders down a mountainside echoed across the land.

"The suon of the glaciers," Raka said beside him.

He turned to the man. He didn't feel the cold, even as a phantom wind pushed their hair around. Raka looked like he had in life, the last few moments they'd spent together. He wore the same Kattakan outfit of hat and woolen coat, beneath which his waistcoat and shirt were buttoned to the throat.

"Why won't you leave me alone?"

Raka met his stare. His dark eyes reflected no light

and the absence of any glimmer sent a shiver through Lilley. It was like looking on the eyes of the dead.

"Because you need to take me home." Like his eyes, there was little evidence of life in the flat tone of his voice.

"You can't get there yourself?"

But Raka looked away from him, back out toward the snow-covered tundra.

He grabbed the man's shoulder. "Raka!"

The snap of his voice cracked the scene and he found himself sitting in Méka's mata, his hand clutching Janan's shoulder instead. Nausea rose at the back of his throat. Méka knelt beside him, touching the side of his face.

"I'm all right," he mumbled. The shapes and scent of the mata seemed to configure into codes he couldn't quite translate fully. A language he wasn't fluent in. But as they didn't usher him to move, he allowed the meaning to infiltrate in slow waves. The stove he'd sat around dozens of times, taking tea and stew. The elk hide he'd skinned, cured, and softened as a gift to Méka upon the new construction of her mata. The aroma of honey and peppermint still lingering in the air. The details of family. "I'm all right," he said again, on a stronger breath.

This time they seemed to believe him. Janan pressed their foreheads together for intimate confirmation. Neither of his companions asked further. They'd heard him shout the culprit's name.

He was disappearing into his dreams.

A Covenant of Ice

*   *   *

IT TOOK SOME gentle patience to wait for the big mata to fill up with all hundred-plus members of the patched together families that resided in this valley of Mazemoor. All had fled from the island north, where now the Kattakans ruled. The majority of the people were of the family Suonkang, as they'd been the first to settle here en masse after the war, but all five Greatmothers of the five Ba'Suon families encamped in the Antler Mountains counseled equally in matters of import. A visit from an agent of Internal Security and her Ba'Suon companion worked a common discomfort through the gathering. Lilley couldn't feel it like Janan or Méka but the looks of concern and restless, milling bodies told the tale.

Gherijtana ele Railé lurked at the periphery of the gathering, but in clear view of where Lilley sat beside Janan, Janan's sister Prita, and Méka and her family. The boy's small stature and enclosed body language still managed to leave six feet of empty space around him in every direction, as his fellow Ba'Suon seemed to adopt the same impression as Méka and Janan upon first meeting him. Even if the wider camp didn't know of the boy's enastramyth tendencies yet, they probably felt it—a wrongness amidst the living nature so endemic to every Ba'Suon's understanding of the world.

Weapons weren't allowed in the big mata. Lilley felt his hand clench and unclench the longer Railé stared across the floor at him.

"What d'you make of him?" he asked the family in his vicinity. Who were now in some manner his companions too, if not his harwan. It had taken Méka's blood family a couple months to warm to him as a Kattakan, unlike Sephihalé ele Prita who'd embraced him immediately and now called him brother, as she did Janan.

Méka's older brother Nai didn't go that far, but they shared a similar persecutory humor. "The family Gherijtana are all notoriously unreliable. Too busy speaking in conundrums to come to any camp with sense."

"Don't judge them too harshly," said Méka's mother, Fari. Her fingers moved nimbly, working leather ties to braid them into reins for dragonback. She looked once in Railé's direction, then to Lilley. "They seek to exist primarily in the flow of the cosmos, which makes them difficult to communicate with. But they've never been unkind to our family, even in the memories of our Greatmothers going back generations." A pointed pause. "You as a Kattakan, on the other hand, might elicit different intentions. His attention on you seems purposeful."

"I been stared at less by hungry wolves, that's for certain."

Ever to the point, Méka's father Iroheem said, "Whose mata will he sleep in tonight?"

Nobody had an answer to that, and nobody who heard the question around them volunteered.

"Railé's with the Mazoön," said Méka. "We'll see

A Covenant of Ice

how he interprets kindness, whether as a Ba'Suon or a Mazoön. Then we can decide where he'll sleep."

"We'll get words from him one way or another," Janan said, "and for all I care he can sleep with the goats." That punctuation put an end to the conversation.

All thought about it receded anyway as the Suonkang Greatmother spoke, the resonance of her voice cutting through the quiet conversation bubbling in the big mata. She sat in the center by the tallest poles. Her white bristle of hair partially obscured the indigo tattoos swirling along her head. Her eyes were the same deep blue as the ink, almost black. They glittered with a sharp awareness and even as the only Kattakan in the assembly, Lilley felt her calm power permeate the entire space. "Suonkang ele Méka has called this council. It seems we were visited early this morning by an agent of Mazemoor."

This news provoked a resurgence in conversation, but it quelled as Méka unfolded to her feet to join the Greatmothers at the center of the floor. She recounted Phinia Dellerm'el's words for all to hear. The dead silence at the news of Kattakan intent in the far north blanketed the entire mata. There were endless machinations from the Kattakans, and now more from the Mazoön upon whose compassion they all relied. Tension eeled through the mata and the eyes of the adults settled on him and Janan. He, the Kattakan, and both of them ex-soldiers, a reminder of the warring violence that existed like a membrane around the living Ba'Suon families.

"They approached Sephihalé ele Janan foremost," said the Suonkang Greatmother. "What can we expect if you and your battle suon refuse their request?"

Janan gestured once across the mata to Railé. "Ask their representative."

The boy was staring up at the ceiling, intricately painted with a scene depicting the paths of the family Suonkang: mountains, grasslands, rivers and forests. And the dragons who watched over them since the beginning of their time on Ishia. The winged figures were splashes of bright colors with golden edges to detail the creatures' scales, artistry to rival any Kattakan inkwork. The Gherijtana seemed oblivious to the whole mata's interest, so focused was he on the painted canvas.

Méka called his name. The boy looked at her with such delayed regard that it could've been more impudence than distraction. They waited. Then the boy said, "It doesn't matter. You'll go north, as the stars deem it." And he made the sign toward the cosmos, but it, too, read like a silent sardonic statement more than a gesture of respect.

"Why are you so certain?" said the Suonkang Greatmother.

"Because I've seen it in a dream. My Greatmother bade me come south to fulfill this dream."

Murmurs rolled through the mata. Lilley watched Méka's frown deepen. She, too, had been plagued by a dream that sent her north as far as Eastern Kattaka, and there they'd met and all the avalanche of Raka's

A Covenant of Ice

actions tumbled down on their heads. Nothing good, as far as he was concerned, came from such dreams.

"Your Greatmother told you to come to Mazemoor because of this dream?" said Méka.

"It's so."

"What exactly did you dream?"

Railé looked at her, then to each of the Greatmothers. "The clarity of that is for my Greatmother and I. To hear more thoughts on it would muddy the vision." He chewed the inside of his cheek as he considered some avenue of dialogue, then looked directly at Lilley. "Also, it would serve to alert this one's companion, Abhvihin ele Raka, if I spoke further of my dream."

The mata erupted with voices and they all seemed to reverberate in his head. Vaguely he felt Janan touch his arm but instead of an anchor, the contact crackled like lightning and rolled through his entire body.

"Na," he said, even if he wasn't sure what he was negating. Not until he felt the force of presence flood his chest.

What did you see, Gherijtana ele Railé?

HE'S LEARNED AFTER Fortune City that the world is thinly layered. The people he calls family, that he calls *love*, are as invisible to touch as any other aspect of nature. He can pass the thought of his hand through the bark of trees as through the air he once breathed, and so the body of the one he silently calls beloved is as water to the net of his desire. He watched the sun rise and set for countless turns and marveled at the brush of color that painted his awareness. He *became* a sunrise, a sunset, like he became the call of the diamondback suon and the running thoughts of this red-haired Kattakan whose eyes he looked through with the same wonder as he looked through the eyes of the king, of an elk, of a hawk wheeling in the sky. The barrier he had lived with since leaving the far north is, in the end, just another insubstantial veil meant to be pierced. No more does he have to exist in the nothingness of a void. When he finally finds home in this Kattakan, he stays.

He isn't alone anymore.

He sits with Lilley on the snow-dusted rocks created by the recession of ancient glaciers. Together they watch the wind cut lines through the winter tundra. The Kattakan is confused, frustrated, but he knows Lilley has never known true peace, not even with his beloved Janan. If he had, they would not have dreamed so ardently of white sands and running away.

"When we go home," he says, turning to look at Lilley's profile, "you'll see."

The Kattakan doesn't look at him. The temperatureless wind courses through his red hair and seems to scour the color from his blue eyes into an almost transparent gray. "You can't keep doin this to me."

"It distresses you because you're fighting it."

"I'm fightin it cause *you* distress me. You're supposed to be *dead*."

"Did you want me to die, Lilley?"

"That's not what I mean."

A Covenant of Ice

"Then help me. Don't leave me like this."

He's not prepared for the intensity of the Kattakan's voice. It crashes against the land from horizon to horizon, against the air like the air is made of glass.

And his world shatters.

GO BACK TO THE STARS LIKE YOUR ANCESTORS.

THE BIG MATA was so silent that even the soundless globe of it created a pressure against his ears. As if the lack of something could also possess mass. He heard nothing from the dragon overhead, either, and when the faces of his companions materialized into his vision, they were as motionless paintings smudged with bleeding colors.

But then Janan seized the sides of his face and the world hardened like iron. Hot to the touch. "Lilley. *Lilley.*"

"I'm here." How often had he been forced to declare that? When those around him showed such doubt? And he couldn't blame them. He doubted himself.

"You see why I can't divulge every piece of my intent," said the Gherijtana. "The Kattakan isn't wholly in control of himself, and we all know Abhvihin ele Raka's propensity for destruction."

That shoved the silent mata into another tidal wave of voices. Frantic bursts of worry boiled to the surface. Even in his daze he felt it. But the Suonkang Greatmother held up her hand to calm the tumult.

"He claims that he's an enastramyth," Janan said, his grip now a vise around Lilley's arm, while his other hand flicked in the foreign Ba'Suon's direction. "Might that also have something to do with why you can't tell us your agenda?"

"Your distrust is understandable," said the boy, "but unfounded in my case. I'm here to help your mission. And to emphasize that going north is the only way."

Lilley forced the voice from his throat. "That's what Raka claims too."

"We can't trust Raka," Janan said. "Or you, Gherijtana. Your mythicism relies on deception and binding nature to unnatural shapes."

"That's your opinion," Railé said.

"That's my *experience*."

"Peace," said the Suonkang Greatmother. "We don't take lightly the words of your Greatmother, Gherijtana ele Railé, but nor do we adhere to the directives of these Mazoön who insist on a manner of knowing that we don't understand."

"Then perhaps you should try to understand it," Railé said. "With respect, Greatmother."

"This country corrupts our knowing," Janan said.

"Your experience here isn't the extent of all truth, Sephihalé ele Janan."

"That may be so, but you're not coming with us if we go north."

"Peace," said Greatmother, and the other four silent Greatmothers all turned to look at him and Janan. They brought a reminder of the war with them and a

A Covenant of Ice

certain pervasive strain. The Greatmothers may have understood Janan's history in this country, maybe they'd seen visions of it, as they'd welcomed him and his battle dragon. But even patience had a limit in a camp when the collective good was at stake and all members of the families shared a unified unease in a way he couldn't feel. When all of nature felt out of its order, Méka had once explained to him.

Lilley reached to touch his harwan's leg, unsure whether he wanted to stop the debate, push himself to rise, or assert some course of action he had yet to fully comprehend. He felt the king dragon now, somewhere over the lake, an insistent pull that seemed attached to the cavern of his chest. It strangled all thought of protest from his throat.

A hand slid under his arm. He looked to his left and met Méka's eyes.

"You still see his home," she said. It wasn't a question and it cut through the murmurs of the council.

"Yeah."

"Maybe it's not a wrong idea to take him there."

"The king dragon?"

"All of him. Raka." She squeezed his arm. "Isn't it all of him that abides?"

"But the Mazoön want us to secure more land for their reaping," he said. "Goin north would ensure that."

"It won't matter what they want," said the Gherijtana boy.

"And why's that?" Janan said.

The enastramyth said, "Raka knows. He wishes to rebalance our world."

The Suonkang Greatmother raised her hand again before more questions arose. "The Mazoön agent wasn't wrong about one thing: if we don't go to the far north, the Kattakans will. The more seasons pass, the more they develop their weapons and their strategies, and maybe with such development they also lose their memories of war and consider it an acceptable risk in disagreement. We can't remain here and think these things aren't happening, and perhaps sending Sephihalé ele Janan to the far north will curtail some of the Kattakan intent without encouraging another conflict."

"He ain't goin alone," Lilley said, "if there's any goin to be had." Beyond any insistence from a dead man or his dragon, this was his resolve. Janan's hand folded around the leather binding his stump and that brought more of himself back inside the mata. Dimly, the diamondback alighted on the lake, the image of the camp's numerous mata from the dragon's perspective forming a film over his present vision. The same resolve powered through the blood of the creature's heart and he settled, wings folding back.

"We spoke of this before in council," Greatmother was saying. "What more might be required of the families to preserve the land. The far north is also a part of the paths of the Ba'Suon, even if a family no longer crosses there. We have a responsibility to the suon of the glaciers, and to all of nature, as the stars deem it."

A Covenant of Ice

"It's decided then," said Janan.

"I'll go as well," Méka said.

Lilley drew a breath. It moved easier through his lungs. The Suonkang Greatmother dismissed all in the big mata, except for the three of them; even the Gherijtana was waved outside. Méka rose to her feet to say a few quiet words to her family before they, too, exited the shelter. The door shut and what warmth that had gathered from so many close bodies now seemed to drift up through the hand-holes in the ceiling. Méka rejoined them on the floor.

The Suonkang Greatmother looked at them, a handful of heartbeats that she didn't break with words. The four silent Greatmothers hadn't moved, but their eyes faced the same direction, unconnected to the material details of the mata. Lilley shivered and looked away.

"We, too, have experienced dreams from the flow of the cosmos," said the Suonkang Greatmother. "The Gherijtana isn't wrong."

"What does it mean?" said Méka. "Rebalancing the world?"

The old woman's deep eyes speared Lilley through. "You and your suon Raka. Even Abhvihin ele Raka. He created a wave the moment he came south from the frozen land of his ancestors. That's what we've been seeing. But the end is unclear."

"What d'you mean, a wave?"

"He'd been years in southern Ishia," Janan said. "And now another year dead."

"In the motions of the cosmos," said Greatmother, "years on our paths are merely a single blink amongst the stars. Perhaps in his current state of being, Raka, too, moves in this manner. We believe his decision to leave his home after the destruction of his family became the beginning of this. We believe a reckoning with the Kattakans on our land is imminent, though we can't see the details or the outcome." Her vein-lined hand reached to grasp Lilley's. "For some reason he chose *you* to see to the end of it. Or so suggests the Gherijtana."

"Nature will rebalance itself," Méka said. "But nature can be tumultuous."

"It's so," said Greatmother. "And Raka in his very being is a force of nature. This is what we can discern now."

"Everything Raka touches ends in ashes," Janan said, the anger and stress flayed open in his words.

And Lilley couldn't soothe it. The pain would repel him, when for years he and his harwan had only drawn closer to each other. Nothing of Greatmother's grip penetrated beyond this pain.

And now the king dragon turned his back on the camp of the families, drawing his attention to the mountains and the brightened day beyond. Lilley felt the pull of that interest until the scene of the big mata began to break apart like a hammer fallen upon a piece of pottery. Until every shard lay scattered on the ground and all he saw were the jagged edges of the horizon to the north.

The dragon launched himself into the sky with a bellow, and they were airborne.

THE ACHE IN his chest was something beyond loss. Like waking from a dream knowing nothing of his strange sleeping life had ever been his own. Wind hurtled through him and forced him back around to face the oncoming horizon. The bruised blue slit of it like a rotting wound.

It wasn't his own loss he felt. Like this wasn't his own body flinging through the sky.

You let me go, Lilley.

You're trying to let me go even now. You won't let me in. You never let me show you.

"Show me *what?*"

But silence. And in that swallowed void, even with wide open eyes fixed on the dark line of the ocean, he saw his mother on a rugged green landscape. Her back faced him as she stared across iron blue waters of a rippling bay. A tangle of thick red and green kelp was strewn at her feet like the discarded locks of a beached mermaid. Like her own hair, scarlet and coiled and blowing in the northern wind.

He didn't want to see this. But these weren't his eyes, this wasn't his vision.

Long ago he'd told Raka of his slave life. Of his mother. He should've known the man would fling it back on him like a form of revenge.

Now Clarra turned toward him. The edge of her

pale cheek, the curve of her jaw. He could see even the fringe of her auburn lashes before she faced him fully and there it was, like it was that night in the courtyard of the masters' villa.

The blood ran down from the gunshot in the middle of her forehead, carving her face with tributaries of viscous red.

We're born from the same pain.

It was night when he opened his eyes. Lamplight danced with shadows in the corners of the small mata. His and Janan's. His harwan sat beside him on the bed and Lilley stared up at the way those shadows carved fine features into luminous shapes. Inside this familiar enclosed space lived silence, but something of his blood still roared, echoing the intentions of the dragon that sat by the lake again, a stone's throw from their mata and as close as his own heartbeat.

Janan touched his chest, over the necklace of red and gold dragon scales. "You went away again."

"Sorry."

"No sorry. Just worry. And your eyes…"

"What about my eyes?" His voice was hoarse, as if he'd been the one bellowing over the mountain peaks. He covered Janan's hand with his own and marked how the other man's gaze fell to the harwa around his wrist. The symbol of their bonding. Belonging to all, beloved of one. A month after Janan had returned to him, they'd performed the ceremony before all the

A Covenant of Ice

scattered families here. Spoke oaths beneath the stars that would never be revoked. He'd accepted the harwa to wear, an artifact passed down through generations of Janan's blood family. He hadn't removed it since, but even its welcome weight of dragon bone and sea pearl was distant now.

"I didn't recognize you," Janan said, with no attempt to hide the upset in his voice.

He pushed himself to sit.

"I can't help you, Lilley. All these months and he's still got a fucking hold on you no matter what we—"

"Na." It was only one word, and it was probably ineffective, but he said it anyway and pulled his harwan closer. "I'm here. I'm fightin."

Janan leaned away from him. Resistant. "But is it working?"

He flushed like a fire had suddenly leapt up between them. Or an unbidden shame.

"Now he's speaking to you. First the visions of the far north, the king suon in your mind, and then you say—"

"You're right." The force of his assertion quelled the litany of his chaos. "I'm fightin but it's a losin war. And now we're goin north with it and that's what *he* wants. And I dunno what I'll end up bein by the time we get there and I'm scared. Maybe I don't come back."

Now it was Janan's denial. "No."

"We don't know what to do cause maybe there ain't nothin to be done."

There were no more words of reassurance. That realization darkened Janan's eyes and the shadows seemed to grow a weight and gather around them until the comfort of their mata became a crevasse from which they could not extricate. The walls just pressed against his shoulders, around his heart. Months of pushing off the truth and grasping after alternatives. Now they sat and instead of the grip of their hands, he found his stare focused on his absent hand.

In the white tundra with Raka, he'd been whole. As if the war had never happened. As if he'd never met Janan. What if Raka pulled him into that vision and he never woke up? Would he forget this life and the man who embodied it? His beloved. Their golden dragon with the one eye. The dream of their white beach, the opposite of Raka's world.

"Lilley."

"Not yet," he said. To Raka. To the cosmos. Not yet and no more. The blood on his mother's face. How as a child he'd screamed at a wall while she fell before it. Not yet. If words wouldn't imprint hard enough, the cling of his hand would. The squeeze of his arms. The press of his lips to Janan's until their fears disintegrated in the crush of it. "It's me." There was no better way to affirm himself, as much for himself as for Janan. Like this, he could recall his life in full, the part of his life that had started with the years forged between them in love. Some voice infiltrating the back of his head and removing his mind from his wits could not withstand the force. He wouldn't let it. Even if

A Covenant of Ice

he knew whose voice it was and what a bastard Raka could be.

So there was desperation, again, when he freed Janan from his clothes and let the same be done to him. Being completely inside his body in the furious motions of claiming drove out all interlopers. He encouraged a possessive pain that felt more like a violent contest. With bruises he'd feel hours later, so to look upon them would remind him of these moments when he was no one else but himself, and he belonged to no one else but his harwan.

Yet even with the swollen shadows pulsing above him, he didn't know if the blood in his mouth was his own need or the dragon's.

In the depth of night he managed to slip from the mata without waking Janan. He was loath to leave the shared warmth but the sudden sleep he fell into after their love only seemed to recover this alien restlessness. Raka drew him out again, so he dressed and went, wrapped in one of the quilted blankets Sephihalé ele Prita had made for her brother after the ceremony of his harwa. It carried Janan's scent and Lilley buried his nose in the folds as he held it around his body with one hand and sat on the lakeshore. Though Raka wasn't splashing about in the water this time, he was close, somewhere in the mountains hunting.

Lilley'd brought his journal with him and spread it open on his lap. He let go of the quilt, held the charcoal pencil, and tried to sort his thoughts from those of the diamondback. Maybe his fate was inevitable, but he had never been one to lay down in a fight. His hand trembled.

If I can divorce myself from Raka's vision, if I can shout at him in our dream, maybe Méka's right and I...

But the words faded both in his mind and on the paper. When he blinked and reread the sentence, it trailed into a flat line that ran like a crooked river to the bottom of the page where another sentence had been written. One he didn't recall.

The taste of blood on your tongue...

He shoved the pencil between the pages and flung the journal into the lake. The recent memory of his mouth on Janan's shoulder, teeth sharpened in skin, flashed briefly behind his eyes before he ground his fist to his face to drive it out. If Raka sat somewhere behind his shoulder, in his mind, he wouldn't give him the glimpse. "Go away."

"I don't think you're speaking to me, are you?"

He whipped around. Gherijtana ele Railé stood behind him. Lilley stared at him, managed a steady intake of breath, and turned to face the lake again. "I reckon I am now."

The boy didn't take the hint. He sat beside Lilley unasked and folded his hands in his lap. "It started with dreams."

He wished he'd remembered to bring his cigarettes out with him. Or his gun. "What?"

"After Fortune City burned. You started dreaming of the ice north."

"Kid, I ain't in the mood."

"Now he speaks to you."

Lilley gave him a slow look. "Wherever they put you to sleep, you oughtta get on back to it."

"I could help you."

He sustained his stare. Moonlight and shadow commingled across the boy's face. It could be a pleasant face if not for its odd blankness. Like half of the Gherijtana wasn't here. "With what?"

"Your dreams. Or visions. Whatever you call them."

"How d'you know what I dream or see?"

"It's all around you like a mirage that won't fade. Don't they see it too?"

"Who?"

"Your harwan and the Suonkang."

He looked back at the lake's gentle waves. It was impossible to sit in their presence and not wonder what it was like to drown. Or what it might've been like to take this kid and shove his head beneath the dark waters. He didn't even know if the irritation was all his own. "They see enough."

"If you translate your chaos into the right words, you can control it."

"What d'you mean? Just say it plain."

"They can't help you. They don't know how. The Suonkang wants you to analyze it and your harwan wants to alleviate it, but none of that will help you control it. You aren't Ba'Suon. What comes naturally to us in how we sense the world will only be confusion for your Kattakan mind. But mythicism can help you."

"The same mythicism that one'a your kind tried to use to enslave Janan?"

"We aren't all like that. Neither is the mythicism. It's just a tool."

"Guns're tools, too, but they only get used for killin."

"But you don't kill yourself with them unless you mean to. Or you're careless."

He studied the lad's face. The eyes were bold in how they didn't turn away, though there still remained a strange disconnect, like the Gherijtana was looking through him. "What d'you want from me? Cause I tell ya right now, I'm beyond fatigued by the demands of others."

"If you let me, I can help you. Like I said, I can't tell you details at the moment because I don't know how much Raka's infiltrated you and if your knowledge would become his. But if you give me your true name, we can begin."

He laughed. Now he didn't care that he didn't have his gun. He let the stump of his wrist fall out of the folds of the quilt. It would make an effective cudgel. "Na. Na, Janan warned me about this. You ain't gettin that."

"Do you even know your true name? I can help you find it."

"I reckon I know who the fuck I am." He levered to his feet and started to walk back to the mata. He never should've left it. The dragon was nowhere, when

A Covenant of Ice

he could've used the extra force against this strange Ba'Suon and his dire pronouncements. But all he felt of the creature was the heaviness in his limbs, his chest. A second presence he couldn't rein in or be rid of.

"Do you still?" The enastramyth called after him. "Do you know who you are? How much longer do you think you'll survive?"

"Both of you can fuck off," he said over his shoulder as he pried open the wooden mata door. And at least one of them, the living one, obeyed.

He intended to avoid Gherijtana ele Railé until the Mazoön agent was scheduled to return to the camp. It was simple enough to do as the boy was relegated to a shared mata with a small family who lodged at the far edge of the valley. They had a child who was afraid of Raka and so kept themselves far apart. They'd been further still when first he'd arrived in camp with Méka, and this position was the result of months inching closer in each new site the families traveled to through the seasons. He guessed the child sensed nothing from Railé, unlike with the king suon. It was another reminder of how disruptive he could be to the families of the Ba'Suon, and yet they still welcomed Lilley to their fire.

That didn't mean he wouldn't remove himself and the diamondback when the opportunity arose. The third morning since Dellerm'el's visit, Méka suggested they take their dragons on a foray, just the two of them.

Grateful for something to do beyond the camp and the lurking enastramyth, he harnessed a surprisingly agreeable Raka and took flight. He thought Janan was also relieved for the break in their constant worries; his harwan decided to go on a hunt with Prita and Nai, and some of the other wranglers.

Raka appeared to be in a good mood. He winged patterns around Rainfall in a form of flirtation that set Lilley's stomach to reeling and rising into his mouth. Wind screamed through the thousands of scales, throwing all the world into a sonic storm. If his hat weren't cinched beneath his chin and his scarf wrapped around the lower part of his face, he would find it difficult to catch his breath or see beyond the blinding light of the sun at high altitude. As it was, he simply held on, gloved hand locked around the harness rope, and let the dragon dictate their flight path. Méka nudged her silver-gray mount toward a lower elevation, likely to spare him the duress, as Raka followed with a happy roar.

They set down in a mountain meadow in the first stages of decay, presaging the winter to come. Looming above them, the snowy peaks filled out the horizon in all directions. Yet the sun was a jeweled eye falling full upon them and he tilted back his hat only slightly as Raka trod some distance away and pissed his mark, taking his shadow with him.

"The way he flies," Lilley huffed to Méka, sitting on the low grass to regain his energy, "it makes me feel like I'm the one flappin through the sky."

A Covenant of Ice

She smiled and joined him, passing over a waterskin. "But you ride like a Ba'Suon."

"Can't get too used to the altitude though. It ain't for my Kattakan lungs."

They drank in silence for a spell. He tracked the path of a small moth flitting between the sallow yellow blooms of a late perennial.

"Do you think," Méka said at length, "that your people would really war with the Mazoön over the ice north?"

He looked at her. So, they couldn't escape even a single worry after all. "I reckon if they really want what's there."

She frowned. "The High Lord at Diam that we met, and your Lord Shearoji… neither of them seem accustomed to sense. Or peace."

"It ain't inherent in that status of my people."

"Whatever it is Raka wants by going back north, and being with you, some reckoning with the Kattakans as Greatmother believes—perhaps that might be the way to free you."

So intent had he been on the idea that Raka was bent on ruining him, this concept struck like a discordant note on an out of tune piano. It didn't make instinctive sense, yet the instrument need only be adjusted. Had his thinking been wrong all this time? He shook his head. "I don't see how. Not to mention his idea of freedom seems to be divorced from livin life."

"He loved you. Why would he want you to die?"

"Why did he do anythin, Méka? He's drivin me mad

60

and don't seem to give a shit. Maybe he wants me to join em."

I don't want you to die, Lilley.

So swift and quiet came the voice that he was still caught in its words when Méka shifted to sit directly before him. She reached for his hand and the leatherbound stump of his wrist, holding them both. "Would he speak to me?"

Something fluttered in his chest like panic. "I don't know. I don't know if it's even possible."

She doesn't understand.

The shadow of the diamondback fell across them both, seeming to carve a hole across half of the meadow. He looked up. The beast's white belly blocked the sun entirely, the span of his wings darkening the limits of their immediate world. Lilley pulled his hand back from Méka and climbed to his feet. "That enastramyth said he could help me, but I reckon he's in the same delusion as the rest of us."

She frowned. "How does he want to help specifically?"

"Through mythicism. Through knowin my true name. But of course he'd say that." The king dragon bellowed, ringing their ears. The sound agitated even Rainfall, who trilled some yards away and tossed her head. Méka looked over, her discontent deepening in lines between her brows. The pull in his chest drew taut. "At the same time, I feel like there's less'a me, Méka. And what's left, there ain't no reinin it."

She stood to take his hand again. "Then maybe you ought to let the Gherijtana try, Lilleysha."

A Covenant of Ice

"Janan would skin him, he so much as yawns in my direction."

"This isn't your harwan's chaos."

When he met her eyes, she was looking at him straight. Unyielding.

"It's not mine either," she continued, "or Greatmother's, or Tourmaline's. It's yours and Raka's. That's what I've come to understand in the past year. None of us can help it because it doesn't belong to us. We can't hear it, we can barely feel it. We can stand with you in it only for so long, even Janan. I think he knows it, too, and it's driving his fear. His frustration. So we're all unbalanced and the whole camp knows it. The way Ba'Suon know."

"And this is what we're takin to the far north."

"Maybe Gherijtana ele Railé's dream, whatever he saw, is the path through your chaos. Maybe his mythicism is. Maybe it will only make things more confusing. None of us truly know. What I *do* know is remaining here won't move you in any direction but worse. Soon the camp will be back on its path south for the colder months, so it's best that we leave. It's best that we take Raka home."

"And take what comes," he said.

She didn't need to answer him. From the somber look in her eyes, she thought it too.

At least she's right about that.

But the enastramyth isn't to be trusted.

Lilley.

Lilley?

Karin Lowachee

*   *   *

HE KNOWS SOMETHING is wrong when in that state of thought and no-thought he finds himself in the twilight of a tall forest, and he scents a campfire back through the trees. These are the woods near to the family Lapliang in Eastern Kattaka, where once he'd been welcomed by the Ba'Suon on his journey to the Crown Mountains with Suonkang ele Méka and Lilley. It's not his memory, though. He turns and the woman is there, like she had been on that night with the family, offering him goat stew.

He says, "How are you here?"

She takes a step toward him, but he moves back once. So she stops. "When you spoke to Lilley earlier. In the big mata. I felt you there. And just now in the meadow. I need only reach out to find you. The part of you that's this..." She frowns. "This feeling. I'll never forget it."

"I should be flattered."

"Why are you doing this to him?"

The shadows between the trees seem to darken.

"You don't know what it's like to be alone. It's a place beyond death where not even our ancestors will go."

"But you're alone by choice, Raka."

"I didn't choose this storm."

Her eyes are black but in them contain the fullness of life. The possibility of creation and the connective forces birthed within. Her living energy. A bitter reminder of what he can no longer touch except like this. "You aren't your chaos."

"We've had this conversation before."

A Covenant of Ice

"Lilley isn't a part of this, Raka. He shouldn't be."

"You don't understand, Suonkang. Neither does Janan. We're all a part of this chaos. There is no separation. This chaos exists in the cosmos to which we'll return after death, and once in a while, I feel it now, it lowers its head to our world. It opens its eyes in one of us."

"But to what end, this desire to go north and drag Lilley with you? To drive the Kattakans away? To turn the land to ash like you did Fortune City?"

IT CAN ONLY BE HIM. HIM.

It's the diamondback suon, his roar that shakes the trees to their roots and forces the Suonkang to cover her ears and crouch on the ground. The forest strips away and they're on the barrens in a perpetual gray dawn, the dead suon Cottontooth collapsed on the rocks. The king suon sweeps overhead, his shadow encompassing the earth as far as the horizon. Impossibly wide.

"Lilley's the only one who can help me," he says to the Suonkang. At the same time the diamondback swings his head around to show his searing eyes, smoke curling from flared nostrils and from between his fangs. A fixed stare upon the woman who remains on the ground, one hand on the gravel. "He's the only one because any other Ba'Suon couldn't contain what I have to do."

In her eyes she asks why. But he turns his back and walks toward the mountains in the distance, deeper beneath the shadow of the suon's wings. He moves toward the place with no thought. His answer would have been meaningless to her, his sister in the families.

She doesn't know his rage.

Karin Lowachee

* * *

HE SEEMED TO exist now in the thinness of dusk. Not quite the sleep of night, not the wakefulness of day. Raka trapped him in a liminal space, whether he was on dragonback or sitting around the camp's fire for meals. He slept and awoke and sometimes didn't know who he spoke to or where he was. Sometimes he opened his eyes, aware of his hand and body and feet, but looked out onto an icy landscape and heard the echoing roars of the massive crystal dragons skate along the winter tundra like a northern wind.

The king dragon coiled in his chest, impatient to move, one hour a playful creature on the water, the next dropping carcasses of alpine elk and the occasional golden bear in the middle of the camp as a form of bloody encouragement. Or perhaps threat. The Ba'Suon around him and Lilley both seemed to interpret the gifts as something more than a ritual offering. Lilley felt, even in their silence, how much they wanted them both to leave.

Janan tried to lure his focus with talk of the old man's mapbook. They were to mark the islets that seemed to be safe from Kattakan whaling and shipping routes, in order to make their way to the arctic with the least amount of contact, none at all if possible. Together in their mata, lamplight illuminating the whimsical drawings of forest creatures on the walls that they'd inked over the months, Raka's infiltration dimmed somewhat.

A Covenant of Ice

Lilley found himself looking across at his harwan, catching each other in a smile.

When he and Janan had first reunited, they'd delighted in spreading the mapbook as far as it would unfold, beginning at one end and slowly traversing the pages to the farthest drawing some ten feet away, thus encompassing the known world. They marveled at the strange names, neither Kattakan nor Ba'Suon or Mazoön, writ in the hand of a meticulous stranger whose only mark on the work was an inked red stamp in symbols they could not decipher. What stories were contained in these lines that formed borders of land and water? What encounters ingrained in the foreign mapmaker's memory that could not be fully illustrated in this book? Here and there were delicate depictions of various exotic creatures of field and air, even the dragons of Ishia, so they supposed if the adventurer was accurate with the suon, they must have been with the rest of it.

But even in the length and breadth of this work, the result might've been scant compared to the real-life wonders. He and Janan filled in the pictures with their own imaginings. There, far past Mazemoor and the southern tip of Ishia, arising from the eastern edge of the page like a great sun, was the upper curve of a seemingly massive land mass that had been labeled *Sirra Kusa*. Mysteriously, no more of this place was depicted; instead, the cartographer had concentrated their focus toward the sprawling ocean and the continents and countries beyond.

He and Janan began to think of this Sirra Kusa as their land of white sand and long sunsets. Every time they looked on the fine drawings, he thought of it. Sirra Kusa. He was traveling north when he should've been going south with his harwan. But when Janan smoothed out the pages to the cartographer's intricate depiction of the islands of Ishia, there was no time to peruse their fantasy. He met Janan's eyes for a brief moment and the subtle curve at the corner of his harwan's lips told him that he, too, remembered. And maybe their future in this possibly mythical Sirra Kusa wasn't entirely shattered against the rocks of external powers. For the first time in weeks he felt a subtle lightness.

They found on the map a chain of smaller islands for possible resting spots that swung away from Eastern Kattaka. The cartographer had labeled the ragged shapes as Widow's Tears, likely, Janan said, because the waters would be rough and many ships must've dashed upon those shores. At the northernmost island, the land of Raka's family, a bay carved into the southeastern border like a great dragon had taken a bite out of the tundra. That was their ultimate destination, to fly over the waters and alight on the shore. It would be the easiest location for landfall for the Kattakans too, should they in fact make it that far as the Mazoön feared.

Looking at the dark lines on the crinkled paper, some of his persistent unease raked fingers through his chest again. Raka, man and dragon, surged once more in his

A Covenant of Ice

body with murmurs and a demand for motion. New images overlayed his vision as he stared at the map.

In this season the bay ice would be thickening to join the land as an almost impenetrable mass. Some of the floes knocked against each other, sounding like sonorant windchimes. He breathed and smelled the vestiges of deep freeze and the congregation of sealflesh as the animals were wont to lay aboard the floes. Maybe the only way to ward against these memories that weren't his own was to close his eyes. Exhaustion sank in its teeth and he was chewed up from it.

Together they packed away the mapbook with the rest of their belongings that they'd separated to take north. Then Janan wrapped him up with both arms and they lay in their bed, saying nothing. He blinked slowly at the cavorting images of their drawings— foxes and rabbits and a bushy-tailed squirrel that Janan claimed was a cat. Creations from the early days of their reunion when it had been much easier to laugh.

Now when he faded to sleep, it was never quite oblivion.

THEY FIND EACH other on the edges of a battlefield. He watches Lilley slowly ease down on a rock overlooking the churning waters far below, where bodies float and crash against the feet of the cliff in such numbers they seem to create a beach of blood and limbs. Some are Kattakan, some Ba'Suon, some Mazoön enastramyths. A couple are battle suon, their long necks and wide wings cracked and splintered like trees felled by lightning strike. A soft golden light still permeates the dark waves, vestiges of the mythicism wielded against their forces. Repelled by the Ba'Suon who fought in the Kattakan ranks. Lilley sucks on his cigarette like it can give him breath. Raka folds down beside him and holds out his hand. They share the smoke.

"Where's Janan?" he asks.

"He needed alone time with Tourmaline."

Raka nods like he understands. In truth, he's relieved to find the Kattakan soldier by himself for once. They watch the red sunrise peel back the night sky. Lilley taps his ashes on the brown grass soaked by rain from a storm just hours before. They're both still wet but it doesn't seem to matter.

"Nothin but carnage," Lilley murmurs.

Raka looks at his profile. He removes his hat and the ends of his red hair, curling from moisture, whip stiffly in the breeze. "It's the world."

"It don't gotta be."

He wonders what it's like to possess such determined hope in the face of this evidence—that every land will lead to this destruction in one way or another. Even his own people weren't immune, but he hasn't exposed that secret to this Kattakan. He is himself death incarnate, but this man, blind and deaf to knowing, sees only a comrade. It's a relief, even a release, to be near to such a person. The absence in his core seems to float like suspended dust, rather than forming a fist of balled energy that resounds against the presence of every Ba'Suon he meets. Like Sephihalé ele Janan.

A Covenant of Ice

"What would you do to fix it? This carnage?"

Lilley's quiet for some time as he smokes and lets his thoughts traverse the pathways of his experiences. Raka watches the memories flicker and shine behind his eyes. Some that conjure a film of tears that don't fall, others that soften the pale angles of his features.

"Maybe I wouldn't fix it," he says eventually. "Maybe I'd just leave."

"Leave the army?"

"Leave Kattaka."

"And go where?"

Lilley lets him have the last inch of the cigarette and tucks his hands beneath opposite arms. Like he's trying to keep his ribs from bending open. "My mother knew to go. Even if she never made it. When your enemies wanna stop you from a thing, then maybe that thing's the thing to do, yeah?"

"What if that thing gets you killed? Like your mother?"

Something in the question makes the Kattakan laugh. The grim sort endemic to soldiers. He doesn't laugh. Lilley looks at him sidelong. "You worried about me, Raka?"

"No."

"Don't be. If I go anywhere, I'll take you."

His heart comes alive in his chest with such fervor it hurts. An ache so encompassing he can't swallow. Yet he doesn't want it to stop. He can move through the world like this if only Lilley repeats those words until the last light fades between them. "And Janan?"

"Course Janan. And Tourmaline too."

The pain twists like a knife. "Janan won't want me."

A crease appears between Lilley's brows. "Why d'you say that?"

Because he sees me. "Because he wants you for himself."

Lilley laughs again. "Na, that ain't how he views things. He's got no reason to rein me when we're both wild."

"What if we left now?"

"What d'you mean?"

"I can take you anywhere you want." He's forgotten the cigarette. It burns the ends of his fingers and he drops it in the wet grass.

"I'm too tired to walk anywhere, Raka. Or ride a horse. I'm gonna need a dragon just to get me up off my ass."

"We won't need a horse or a suon."

"What're you talkin about?" A smile lingers on Lilley's face, one of amusement and gentle affection. Somehow this Kattakan can still be gentle. With him.

Then Janan's voice slices through the dull air behind them. Raka stares as Lilley turns to greet the Ba'Suon man, his smile stretching wide like the dawn. Light all gold and lavender burnishes every ragged edge on Lilley's face and reflects nothing but shadow onto his own heart, which has grown silent except for a stabbing, hollow pain.

Pain and anger and the destruction that has become his kin.

THE AGENT RODE into camp a day early. He and Janan and Méka were trying to affix the harness ropes onto their dragons. Naturally Raka decided to be contrary and this set off the other two, even staid Rainfall, who chuffed and ducked behind Tourmaline's rear like she was playing hide and seek with Méka. He shoved Raka's face—the dragon was trying to eat his hat—and watched as Gherijtana ele Railé approached Dellerm'el and the two of them spoke out of earshot for a few minutes. Then Dellerm'el looked over at them, ignoring the beasts, and dismounted. She handed the reins to the boy and walked up to meet them, a look of sober business in the tight pinch of her mouth. What had been a simmering tension behind his eyes now began to pulse with a throbbing pain.

"Somebody die?" he asked her.

She looked at Janan, ignoring him. "Well?"

"We're going," Méka answered instead. "All three of us."

"Good. My enastramyth will accompany you. This isn't up for debate. If you're prepared, you can leave by nightfall. Your dragons can navigate in the dark, can they not?"

"What's the hurry?" Janan said.

Lilley clenched his fist, where his blood seemed to freeze his hand into a hard ball. The scent of ice pricked his nostrils and he looked at the king dragon, who angled an unblinking yellow eye at him. The agent was still speaking.

"…reports have placed a Kattakan whaling ship and a couple corsairs en route to the northern waters. They must believe we have wind of their forays and they want to head off any of our own incursions without looking like they're forming an armada. Hopefully

Karin Lowachee

they won't expect riders on dragonback. But to be on the safe side, you're to avoid them and any islands currently claimed by Kattaka. They may interpret any landfall as an act of war."

Lilley said, "The northern dragons might interpret their presence as an act of war."

Dellerm'el's gaze pinned on him finally. "Why do you say that?"

He couldn't answer her. The words had fallen out of his mouth with no thought. At least none of his own. The silence even amidst his companions sounded pointed; only the queens paced and chuffed at each other, while Raka's baleful gaze searched the skies northward. Nobody wanted to explain his chaos to this woman and maybe she felt some silent understanding amongst them that she couldn't access. Her eyes narrowed at him, but Janan drew her attention back.

"We're ready. We just have to load our suon."

"They'll be able to withstand the frigid temperatures?"

"They will take us as far as they can," said Méka, "and we'll see."

The agent rubbed her chin with a gloved hand, the dissatisfaction plain.

Lilley gestured to the Gherijtana. "He ain't ridin on our dragons though."

"I won't need to," said the boy, and walked off. The horse he'd been holding stomped nervously when Raka's attention swung that way. Lilley moved to soothe the animal but she shied from him and walked

A Covenant of Ice

backward until Méka touched her neck and spoke quietly against her cheek. Blood thudded through his ears and for a moment his vision doubled, red shadows infiltrating the scene—Janan's attempts to refuse the enastramyth from coming on the journey; the Mazoön agent's dismissal of his protests. Lilley seemed to hear his harwan's heartbeat kick up a pace, or maybe it was the nervous horse. He looked toward the lake, his vision from Raka's height as the dragon swayed his head back and forth, scenting the air.

Leave it alone, he wanted to tell Janan. If for no other reason than because Raka didn't want the boy around.

Apparently, the kid had disappeared in order to do his magic in private. Nai and Prita interrupted their second attempts to harness their mounts and reported that the Gherijtana was performing some mythicism rite on the edge of the camp and the other Ba'Suon were starting to grow uneasy. The agent said some general words of reassurance, as if that would assuage them or somehow command them, but nobody listened to her. In minutes they arrived at the northern front of the camp. Gherijtana ele Railé was crouched on the ground holding a couple of black rods half the length of a man's arm. In his other hand was some sort of metal pick. Or maybe it was a needle. He was scratching into one of the rods with the needle. As he did so, a glowing yellow line formed in the needlepoint's wake.

The sound of blood began to roar in Lilley's ears. He

set his hand on the grip of his gun, but Janan pulled one of his blades, disregarding the small wave from Méka to tell him to hold.

"What are you doing?" Janan snapped.

Railé kept making those glowing lines on the rod, unperturbed by the presence of any weapon or the congregation of his boss and others. "I'm calling my suon since that king won't let me ride him."

"You don't make your mythicism in this camp," Janan said. "Stop it now."

Méka said, "Explain what you're doing. What are those marks?"

"No," Janan said. "Suonkang. Those markings trap the world with words. You don't know what he's capable of." He set the edge of his blade to the boy's neck. "I said stop."

Even Dellerm'el didn't protest. She watched the Ba'Suon in her midst and the obsidian shine of Janan's blade. Lilley breathed the tension and it came to him with the scent of blood. Along with the image of his mother, her back to a stone wall, the ivy crawling like capillaries along its surface. He blinked and it was the boy again, motionless beneath Janan's blade.

Slowly, Railé set down the rod with its glowing sigils, and the bare one, and the needle beside them on the grass. With hands raised he levered to his feet.

"Explain," said Méka.

"The markings represent the essence of intent. I call my suon by evoking his name and my intent into the conduit."

A Covenant of Ice

"And the suon has no choice," Janan said.

Railé looked at him from the corners of his eyes, like he was trying not to startle a deer. Then he looked at the agent and some silent word passed between them. "He has choice. Not all usage of a name is for compelling, regardless of your experience with Eben Wisterel."

Janan's blade hand shifted at the sound of that name. They all knew it. The boy didn't do himself favors by conjuring it now. "You're not helping yourself."

"I'm only saying the truth."

Méka said, "Next time, you tell us before you work your mythicism. We need to trust one another on this journey, do you understand?"

Overhead, the roar of an incoming dragon echoed across the northern face of the Antler Mountains. The camp's crown set up a ruckus of reply. Closer on the ground, Raka bellowed to drown out all smaller calls. There could be no trust. The fact the dragon and his harwan aligned in their opinion of the enastramyth felt both foreign and wrong. When had Raka and Janan agreed on anything in the end? Hesitant acceptance had soured into suspicion once more and he recalled the buffeting from both sides. Now Raka wanted him to remember his life in Diam, and Janan sought to shelter him from mythicism. Both realities collided like ice flocs on shifting water. Either way he was trapped and his elbowing to free himself from the onslaught sent tremors of nervousness and trepidation through the sensitive knowing of all he called family.

Karin Lowachee

The Ba'Suon amplified the feeling in one another so that even he could sense it pummeling against his skin.

"We have to go," he murmured, but nobody was listening. Janan had dropped his blade from the boy's throat but one more word in any direction threatened to galvanize another debate.

"Railé is going to relay reports to me using this mythicism," said the agent, proof enough that she sensed none of the turmoil or perhaps just didn't care.

Lilley looked around for something to sit on. A rock nearby provided the spot and he took up residence. Some of his headache abated or at least sitting in one place provided no energy to feed it. All around him flares of heat flew: Janan, Méka, their family in Prita and Nai emboldened to try to protect what they knew and control what they didn't. And something in the clamor seemed to satisfy Raka. The dragon's presence hummed steady and strong through his limbs, calmed by the chaos. While he watched, he pulled his roll papers and pouch of tobacco from his pocket and began to do the only thing that made any sense in the moment. The focus at least steadied his hand.

Without so much as a greeting, the Gherijtana sat beside him on the rock and leaned to peer into his face. Lilley swatted him away, stuck the rolled cigarette between his lips and lit it with a struck match.

"Let me show you," the boy said. "Let me help you."

He spoke around the smoke. "Not if you need to hear my name from my mouth, you won't."

"I don't for this."

A Covenant of Ice

Lilley blew some of the smoke in the kid's direction, neither believing nor denying. All argument at this juncture felt like a futile avenue.

Railé's stare drifted to the other Ba'Suon in their vicinity. He pitched his voice. "Suonkang. Sephihalé."

The conversation stopped. Janan walked over at speed like he wanted to shove the Gherijtana off the rock, but Lilley held up his hand with the cigarette and offered it to his harwan to waylay any violence. "He ain't done nothin. Let em speak." He didn't have to look to know the king was lurking near the lake, attention renewed by this fresh focus on the enastramyth. Nearby, their harnesses hanging, Tourmaline and Rainfall paced. The smaller ones of the crown remained on the other side of the camp, wise to keep away where so much felt unsteady.

The enastramyth looked to the agent and she nodded once. They watched as he retrieved the black rods of mythicism from the grass. He held them like Janan and Méka handled their blades, but the Gherijtana carried no blades. Which meant he hadn't gathered his incoming dragon, or any dragon, himself. In this age of scattered families this wasn't entirely rare, but a boy like this, so comfortable in his abilities—it made Lilley wonder.

The black rods hummed with provocation.

"Explain what you're doing every step of the way," Janan said.

The boy said, "I'll build a fire, nothing more. But first I'm going to call my suon again." Needle in hand,

78

he drew those glowing lines on one of the black rods and in minutes they heard a dragon roar from over the north range. Closer than before.

The diamondback bellowed in return and the Ba'Suon who had poked their heads toward this demonstration quickly retreated into their mata, their voices a receding tumble to Lilley's ears. Even the Greatmothers stayed away, perhaps trusting them to handle this Mazoön complication. Or hoping in their absence he and his noisy dragon would leave sooner. Raka took to the air and landed near enough to Lilley's position to cause the ground to tremble beneath the rock. The golden eyes burned in Railé's direction, but Lilley looked up and reached his hand to scrape his fingers over the tent of the broad wing.

Raka's attitude drew Tourmaline closer to their impromptu circle too. She bared her fangs at him and arched back her wings. Janan did as Lilley had and touched the underside of her left wing until the air around them began to smooth. Rainfall had disappeared, but Lilley wouldn't have been surprised if her rider had somehow suggested she remain scarce in the midst of so much instability.

Unlike her dragon, Méka stepped closer, eyes on the glowing rods. "That writing?"

"They're whatever I want them to be," said the enastramyth. "Right now I want them to call the suon."

Janan moved to stand behind the Gherijtana. "Can you do it even if you don't know its true name?"

A Covenant of Ice

The boy glanced up and over his shoulder but turned back to look at Lilley. Like he was the only one who needed to understand this. "In general, yes. A general call. But there's less likelihood he would answer. This way—" He pointed to the sigils he'd made with the needle, "—I can be specific. Think of it like someone calling your name in a crowd, instead of just shouting something without addressing you directly. How likely are you to answer the indirect call? You might look toward its origin, but you wouldn't know it was for you, nor would you care necessarily."

It made a kind of sense. But from what Janan had told him about enastramyths like Eben Wisterel, they were well versed in twisting words to their meaning. Lilley kept watching. The pounding behind his eyes took flight again. "And how're you gonna build a fire?"

Railé gestured up toward the approach of his dragon. The creature streaked in from the long foam of clouds and alighted some feet away, wings fanning. Not for threat, but for pride. The orange eyes angled this way and that as he tilted his head to assess them. The scales were the color of blood and deepened to obsidian around the talons and the tip of the tail. A smaller dragon than the northern kind, as was common among the southern species, but even Lilley felt the beast's attitude in how he attempted to piss his mark on an open patch of grass near to the diamondback.

Raka flung his tail around and forced the red dragon to leap away. The younger one made a high-pitched staccato sound and it took Lilley a minute to realize the creature was laughing in some way.

"Rascal," Lilley said. "That's his name."

The enastramyth boy stared at him as if he'd just pronounced the day of his death.

"The fire," Janan said.

The Gherijtana reached out a hand to stroke the spine of Rascal's red wing and slowly turned back to his black rods and the engraving work upon them. He drew more glowing yellow lines with precise strokes.

"I'm telling these vessels to hold a certain amount of the heat that will hit it from the suon fire, and to release some of it so we can feel the warmth."

Lilley leaned forward, elbows on his knees, and took his cigarette back from Janan. But drawing on it made no difference to the mounting pressure in his mind. "Alla that in them few scratches?"

"If the pattern's elegant, you don't need much." The boy stuck one of the rods into the ground.

Méka crouched close to inspect the markings. "What distance can this calling travel?"

"It depends. For the relay reports Agent Dellerm'el requires on our flight, a specific pattern on it will act as a conduit. Another pattern will be written to give information. She will capture this second pattern so they would know our progress."

"Like those tall silos on the borders," said Janan. "The conduits, as you call them. They caught me when I first came here."

"It's so."

A Covenant of Ice

Lilley knew the boy was waiting for him to ask, so there was no reason to be coy about it. But the words felt like lead on his tongue. "This the way you reckon you can help my chaos? To make this rod drawin?"

The boy looked back down at his sigil work. "After a fashion. Do you know the elements of fire?"

"I reckon flames and heat."

"No. Deeper than that."

"Deeper?"

"What're the flames made of?"

He frowned. "They're made'a flames."

"No, everything has an essence. Everything. The essence of things aren't things we can see or touch. Well... Kattakans can't. Nor Mazoön, they've forgotten. The Ba'Suon, we 'feel' it. We feel everything in nature and sometimes the cosmos above. The Greatmothers understand the cosmos in this manner. For the Mazoön, they have to quantify it through logomyth patterns. Maybe it'll work that way for a Kattakan, too, and once you quantify what Abhvihin ele Raka's doing with you, you might be able to fight it. That's my attempt, anyway."

He grasped maybe every other word the boy spoke, but he gleaned some aspect of meaning from it nonetheless. Spoken with such inevitability, it was difficult to dispute. Especially through the fog of his thoughts. "Méka sometimes calls this... the essence, as you say, the energy of things."

Méka nodded when the Gherijtana looked her way.

"That's one way to name it. So if you can find the pattern of these elements, you can control it through these sigils. Each sigil represents an essential element. If you set the pattern in the right order, in its most elegant and fundamental order, nature will recognize this understanding."

The wind sang. It came through the scales of the three dragons nearby. They had otherwise fallen silent as if they, too, listened to the boy's words. The enmity emanating from Raka coated Lilley's tongue with the taste of ash.

"Nature understands," Janan said quietly, "and you control nature? Through mythicism?"

Railé said, "Yes."

"That doesn't sound right."

"The Mazoön haven't solved *all* logomyth patterns."

"It's still not right. It's like you're trying to make nature obey you. But we covenant with nature."

"Yes. But this is what my Greatmother bid me learn. To understand the world the Mazoön are creating. And this is what I can teach Lilley because his chaos is just another aspect of nature. As Raka was. As Raka is. Even the void of him is a part of the world and the cosmos. If he understood that he might've been able to control it." The boy's gaze flicked up toward the diamondback, who continued to stare. To the Gherijtana's credit, he didn't turn away.

But Lilley stood, a rising tide in his chest. A flooding. As if the enastramyth's words had displaced some part of himself. The king dragon moved to tower over him, over all of them, blocking the sun. Janan said nothing to the boy's claim, but Lilley felt the denial like it was

A Covenant of Ice

armor worn to keep him out as well. His chaos was engulfing them without discrimination and he wanted to walk deeper into the shadow of his dragon.

"Raka was against nature," Janan said.

Railé crossed the second rod against the first, both embedded in the ground. He stood and looked to his dragon and the red beast stepped forward with a chuff. They all moved back. The enastramyth's dragon blew fire onto the rods and the rods caught them and seemed to hold the thick flames as good as any tinder and wood. After some moments the flames grew as if fed by more logs. Warmth bathed their faces with leaping growth.

But looking at his harwan, all Lilley saw was fear. Confusion. Méka's arms folded against her body, a grudging acknowledgment of what they'd just witnessed deepening the focus of her eyes. They watched the fire cavort like it was no different from the cooking flames at the center of the camp.

"Let me try something, Lilley," said the boy. "I don't need your name for it, but it might help you before we leave."

As he stood there, the lulling flames seemed to push him deeper into the dark. He heard his voice as if from beneath the earth. "What?"

"I might be able to dampen Raka's hold on you. I've felt his nature through my dreams and I've been working on a pattern for months to resolve it. I can't explain more than that without getting technical, and you won't understand. But I won't have any control over you, this will just be a logomyth pattern to bind his energy."

He looked at Janan, who shook his head. Méka didn't say anything when he searched her eyes either. It would be his own choice, even as the diamondback stretched to his full height and bellowed, forcing them to cover their ears. The pull in his chest felt like barbed wire around his heart and the urge to climb to the dragon's back began to tremble his limbs.

"Lilley, no," said Janan.

"Do it," he said to the enastramyth.

THE STORY WEAVES through his body like a needle. An incantation, a chant, and the more it repeats, the less solid he becomes.

The absence of light, the deep and forever black, the pull. The center where it all becomes infinite and wanting. The no escape. The swallowing.

The loneliness.

The absence of light, the deep and forever black, the pull. The center.

Infinite. Loneliness.

No escape.

The pull.

Deep.

And the dark.

Alone.

*   *   *

A Covenant of Ice

HE STANDS ON the white tundra. All around him his family. Tall sealskin figures, hunting spears twice the height of his Greatmother. The swarm of sled dogs barking on the ends of their leads. He tastes whale fat in his mouth, and the flesh of char. He tastes blood. The pounding of the white bear's heart echoes at the back of his eyes. In the distance, the ice crown calls, coming in from the hunt. The garrulous beat of wings. The winter of the day casts the world in a permanent twilight.

He can't shut his eyes. In one thought to the next the incessant pulsing in his head climbs to such a pitch that all the cosmos seems to be drumming in the cavern of his skull.

His mother stands on the edge of the floes and turns to look at him. Three black holes form her lidless eyes and open mouth. The red fourth eye in the middle of her forehead.

He can't shut his eyes.

The villa wall bursting like capillaries and the long, strong hands of his father holding his shoulders, keeping him immovable, shoving his scream right down to his feet. So all the world echoes back his grief as long as he walks the earth.

In this white world, where glaciers fall from the impact of echo, he grabs the sides of his hair and screams.

The sky shatters. Twilight breaks apart like blowing snow.

He turns his back on his family. Lilley stands on the edge of the camp, the stark undulation of the land behind his shoulders. But he sees it in the Kattakan's blue eyes like a reflection in water: terror. Confusion. He can't blink and the ashes of his dead family are caught by the cold wind and gusted black between them, engulfing the air.

His family in the ashes, and every sound, every breath, collapses into the void of himself and falls silent.

And the silence is a fist.

THE DRAGONS WOULD not quit roaring in his head. Open eyes revealed a fragmented sky and the world ringing in his ears, all blood and pealing bells. The gray clouds shimmered in his vision like some god had grabbed hold of the dome of the earth and shook it to death. A god was wringing the neck of the sky. Lilley rolled over and the ground shifted beneath him in stutters. Far above him, the size of an eagle at such distance, Raka soared.

"What... what..." His own voice echoed back at him. *Don't don't try to to move move...*

Why why did you let let him do do that to to you?

He blinked at Janan. Méka by his shoulder. Both of them talking but their mouths were out of sync to the words in his mind. Like they weren't speaking aloud at all. Like a dream. The terrible possibility that for as long as he could remember, maybe he was only an apparition of someone else's sleep. Or maybe he was dead already and this was just him trying to remember himself.

"Stop... stop..." He tried to push away their hands. Damp soil and grass beneath his palms. Metallic blue waters in every direction, its own murmuring

A Covenant of Ice

language. Some distance away on the land, the red dragon Rascal with Gherijtana ele Railé on its back, fists wrapped in halter rope. A low rumble seemed to pass between them like the tremor of an earthquake answering another.

All at once Janan gripped his shoulder and turned to the other two Ba'Suon.

"*Leave us alone.*"

The force of it physically propelled Méka back on her feet. Rascal launched himself into the air where Tourmaline circled, crying to the clouded sun.

He blinked and he was kneeling now. In another blink Méka had disappeared. He heard Rainfall call over the water. It was just him and his harwan together on this small island in the middle of the ocean. He could look left and right and see to the edges of it, the slope of rocky beach and straggle grass and a sparse stand of coniferous blue trees. One of them towered directly above him but rather than a sense of protection, the shadows entrenched a kind of menace.

Janan crouched in front of him and held his shoulders. "Lilley. Look at me."

"Why'd you chase em away?"

"Do you even know where you are?"

"With you." For some reason, those two simple words felt like trying to hold onto the waves.

Janan embraced him in a crushing grip. He succumbed to it, the colors of the world slowly bleeding back together. Sounds began to cling to each other and make more sense. He couldn't raise his arms. It was enough just to rest against this man and believe himself whole.

"I thought he'd killed you," Janan said into his shoulder.

"What happened?"

For this, Janan set him back so they could look each other in the eyes. Wind circled them like wolves, growling from the open water. He didn't know why shame knotted in his nerves as Janan took his hand in both of his.

"That enastramyth tried to force him out of you. And it was…"

"What?"

Rings of pink had invaded the whites of Janan's eyes, like he'd knuckled them too often. A certain staring rawness clouded the green irises. "You started to break apart. I don't know how to describe it. Like a part of you was trying to tear itself free. Your eyes from your eyes, your limbs from your limbs. I felt the muscle of your heart twist in on itself. You screamed until the diamondback picked you up in his jaws and brought you here. It took everything for Méka and I to keep you in sight. So we didn't lose you." His voice began to disintegrate. "That *fucking* enastramyth, I *warned* you—"

"I had to try." It was barely him talking. He didn't recognize the sound falling off his tongue. "I had to try somethin or the next time I go away I might not come back, Janan."

"Don't say—"

A Covenant of Ice

"You gotta hear it. And I dunno that the kid is bad. He didn't kill me, yeah?"

Janan tugged his hands away and stood. Like even the thought in his head was poison but he couldn't escape it. The acid nature of it dripped from his tongue and Lilley watched him, feeling the burn. "You can't trust them. The ones that Dellerm'el made me track and find—Wisterel wasn't even the worst of them. That's the whole of it, Lilley. Wisterel was *kind* compared to the shit they had me deal with. People—people using their mythicism to bind others to degradation. To slavery of one kind or another. *Children,* Lill. Animals, people, all of nature—there's no good in any of it, only suffering."

When the torrent stopped they were both breathless. He searched for Janan in the muted center of that hurricane, looking straight at him. He sought the love that had once felt inviolate, but now they were made of glass. Light and care trickled between the cracks and he couldn't grasp any of it. The presence of the king dragon had flung out his wings and arrowed his crest, to the point all Lilley felt was the mass of him. Talons and teeth. An ocean's pressure of the diamondback surrounded him, suspending him in the dragon's own depths.

Harwan.

The word hung between them. The cuff on his wrist felt cold. He searched for Janan, but the thinness of his sanity let the love pass through. His harwan reached for their love in the subtleties of their bond, but he wore this king dragon like armor. He hadn't the strength now to slip it from his own skin.

But we'll go home.

I've waited a long time.

A long time for you.

When the dragons began to return to the island, the other two riders astride, he still didn't move and neither did Janan. Futility drew the boundaries of their intimacy now, created a chasm he couldn't bridge. Méka asked if they were all right. Lilley walked to Raka's outstretched foreleg even before the Gherijtana boy began to speak.

"A ship's anchored off-shore of an island just north of here. Your Lord Shearoji is on it."

Of course the enastramyth was aware of the Kattakan general. None of it mattered. He took up the rope one-handed from around his dragon's shoulders and together he and Raka launched into the growing night.

HE REMEMBERS THE first black ships that touched the ice of his home, how they plowed through the floes like a fist through snow, and the suon cried. He remembers because the suon remember, going back generations in their family lines. So his suon showed him the memories from centuries past, when his ancestors stood upon the white tundra and watched as the black ships entered the frozen bay, piloted by ghosts. Ghost people who gave nothing of living nature, covered in the skin and fur of animals his family didn't

A Covenant of Ice

recognize. These ghosts wielded sharp metals carved with strange symbols, and they spoke a language that sounded as harsh and hollow as their foreign hearts.

The suon didn't wait for the ghosts to attack. In their memory and thus in his own, the crown of the deep glaciers struck through the silver sky and breathed the black ships to ice.

THE KATTAKANS WERE hunting sumara, the suon of the long waters. As he and Raka sailed the skies toward another island in the Widow's Tears, he spied the harpoons on the ship deck and a carcass they'd been cutting up. Bile rose to the back of his throat.

He and his suon settled on a thin stretch of rocky beach at the base of the islet, where cold waves stroked the shore and his boots quickly became wet to the calves. Raka wandered out in the water some yards off but still stood his full height so that the white of his belly remained untouched even by the spray. Slowly his tail curved up and swayed sinuously while his head faced forward and fixed. Soon, Lilley's companions and the Gherijtana alighted nearby with their dragons. Gold, gray, red. A swirl of jeweled colors and the restless energy of a crown whose king sent his impatience out to the cosmos in pulses. But his attention remained on the ships—the Kattakan whaler and two privateers, as the agent had reported.

Lilley couldn't make out the name of the ship, only its crimson Kattakan flag and the open flaps of the gunports. The rest of the vessel was a bruised silhouette against the darkening sky, the setting sun now a lava channel of flame on the longest line of the horizon. Beside him, Méka squinted toward the whaler, where the last lance of light reflected off a steaming scow aimed directly at them. By and by it stuttered to a halt in the shallows. His old general and two sailors jumped from the deck to splash ashore. Rifles remained slung, which was wise. They were ineffective against the suon. Beyond the approaching figures, even he could see without Ba'Suon vision how the ship's cannons were now leveled in their direction, for what good they would do at such a distance. That was where Raka pinned his gaze.

Lord Shearoji's long black hair, once streaked by silver, hung mostly gray now. It had been over a year since Lilley'd laid eyes on the man. His beard had grown completely salt, but his eyes flashed the same piercing iron and stabbed from one to the other, landing lastly on Janan. Yet his voice collected a depth of weariness Lilley didn't remember hearing before.

"I'm surprised you're still alive, Sephihalé."

Janan adjusted his stance, hand on the hilt of one of his blades, as he took stock of the men flanked on either side of the lord. "You and me both."

Shearoji's mouth moved in the semblance of a smile that might have been a strange respect. "I see you've brought your dragon."

Janan didn't answer. Tourmaline scraped the gravel with her talons and angled her long muzzle to regard

A Covenant of Ice

the lord general with her unscarred eye. The sailors shifted nervously.

Lilley said from Janan's right hand, "We got this one too, you may remember him." He gestured up to Raka, who swung his head down to peer at the foreign Kattakans. The diamondback hissed in their direction so his hot breath sliced through the biting sea air.

"I remember," said the lord. A brief glance at Méka, with some clear recollection of their last foray together in and around Diam. But it was as much dismissal as acknowledgment, as if recognizing more than that would somehow jeopardize his composure. His stare drifted back to Lilley. "We saw your dragons. I must admit I'm surprised it's you, considering you worked so hard to quit our country. What exactly are you and your company doing this far out from Mazemoor?"

"Anything we damn well please," he said.

Shearoji took a step closer. Raka snarled, and he stopped. Lilley didn't move, none of his companions did. The general's men shifted and flexed their fingers on their weapons. "You know any attack, whether it's by dragon or gun, would be considered an act of war, Lilley."

The air began to buzz. Or it was something else running through his blood, loud enough he heard it. "You want another war, you'll get one. But it won't be from the Mazoön."

"Meaning what?"

"We know you're goin north. Raka's family come from them islands. And you saw what Raka did."

"Rumor amongst you Bastards claim Raka's family is dead. Just like he is."

Lilley laughed. He couldn't stop it. Not even when he felt how much it disconcerted everyone on that beach. The mild alarm from Méka and the carefulness in Janan. The somber scrutiny from the Gherijtana. He laughed until tears collected at the corners of his eyes.

"What is Mazemoor's intent in the north?" said the general, a dark warning in his tone.

"What's yours?"

"Turn back, Lilley." Shearoji pinned them each with a stare. Even the Gherijtana. "All of you. Take your dragons and be grateful our two nations have reached an understanding. Kattaka in the west doesn't wish to rekindle another conflict, but we will defend our right to this territory and leave you to the south."

"For how long?" said Janan. "Your people don't tend to leave any land untouched."

"This isn't your land to carve," Méka said. "Nor *can* the waters be carved. Do you not understand this?"

Only the enastramyth boy didn't speak. Perhaps because he, too, knew it was futile. Lilley raised his hand to signal to Raka to stretch out a foreleg. He grasped the spine of the king's wing and walked himself up to the whale-length of the creature's back. The dragon shifted until his tail arched up, the sharp end bent toward their enemies.

The hiss of waves filled the sudden silence on the shore. The sailors looked to their lord, then back toward the safety of their ship.

A Covenant of Ice

"If you insist on your path north," Lord Shearoji called up to him, "then I anticipate we'll see you there."

The roar returned to his ears, like his rushing blood contained the vastness of the ocean and the heavens were rumbling above it. Any moment now sheets of storm would veil across his vision and surround them.

THEY WERE FORCED to rest on another islet of the northernmost part of the chain of the Widow's Tears. Nothing more than a rocky growth from the middle of the dark waves, struck over millennia by storms until the granite ran smooth. Tufts of grass and straggle bush adorned the topmost surface like an old man's balding pate. All features of the world came to him like a succession of paintings across his vision. He couldn't touch any part of the texture, there was a frame around the horizon, the moon, the stars, telling him there was nothing beyond that. Just a void. Janan hovered over him as he sat, folded in on himself while his mind tried to bend back to a familiar configuration.

The enastramyth created a fire with his black rods and his red dragon. The heat washed back over Lilley and it was like wearing smoke. Raka pissed his mark and none of the other dragons dared challenge him. He settled behind Lilley, who heard the king breathing and felt the long wings shiver once in a while. The tail thumped the earth like it was counting down to some dire fate. Janan tried to touch him, first his knee, then his arm. Asking without asking, because the answer was the same. *No, I'm not all right. No, I don't know how this will end. Forget about Sirra Kusa. Do you want your harwa back? Would you remove the oaths from the stars, rearrange the constellations so they no longer recognize us?*

He didn't know if these were his questions or just the answers he was given. Méka sat on his left side, where he no longer had a hand, and she poked at the mythicism fire with a stick as if it needed to be stoked, and Gherijtana ele Railé told her not to, to just let the fire be. The other dragons kited over the deep waters, calling their particular song, and it sounded like grieving.

He was sitting between his two companions and yet he was disappearing. He couldn't look his harwan in the eyes because the pain shone too stark. On Méka's face, normally so composed, grew deepening lines of worry and ragged contemplation. It had never been only his chaos. These two people he loved bore the strain of it as continually as their Ba'Suon blades. But what beset him was not something they could wield, and neither could he. Nor was this chaos something any of them had earned.

The rhythmic breathing of the diamondback behind him and the continual strokes of heat from the fire cajoled him to sleep. So did Janan, a hand between his shoulders. He laid his head on Janan's lap, arms tucked in against his chest, and wandered through the fields of shallow sleep while his harwan's fingers

A Covenant of Ice

carded through his hair. The night air echoed with a strange, plaintive refrain.

It could have almost been peace.

THERE'S NO SLEEP. They're sitting on the highest point of the island, the moonlit waves dashing themselves against the granite skirts. Below, the Kattakan ship with its twin escort corsairs cut a trident through the black. They will make it to the bay ice in a day but on dragonback it will only take half that time.

"Our dear lord general doesn't know what he's going to meet," he says to Lilley.

"Will you do to him what you did to Fortune City?"

"Is that what you fear?"

Lilley leans over as if preparing to drop off the side of the cliff. "I'm afraid of so many things I lost track, Raka."

"You don't have to be afraid with me."

"So you're gonna leave me after this?"

"Is that what you want?"

His Kattakan doesn't answer.

"I won't burn the ships."

"But you want destruction."

He looks at Lilley's hands. The untouched left and the dynamic right, how even in this state it can hold his breath. Like this man was the evergreen, the leaf and the palm, that filled and stopped his lungs.

"I want *justice*."

"You want revenge, Raka. To be consumed by somethin other than this void. But you're consumin *me*."

The air shivers around the words. The light on the long waters seems to coalesce and dance in accusatory patterns. Of course he wants them to succumb to the waves, to become a part of a force so vast and constant it can break even rock. "If you let go of yourself with me," he says to the water, or the water says to him, to them, "you'll be free."

But Lilley doesn't reply. He sits frozen, not even breathing. As if someone's cast his image in stone and set him here like a sentinel.

"Lilley?"

Then he hears the voices. The Gherijtana enastramyth. The Suonkang and Sephihalé. All of them talking and Lilley asleep somewhere beyond this nowhere place, listening.

...to lead the ice suon to Kattaka.

And do what?

What they will need very little cajoling to do. They've done it before to every ship that has gone to their shores. But it won't be like Fortune City. It will be every city.

Surely not even Raka...

No?

That was your dream?

It's so. And Lilley is the vessel, the same way mythicism requires a vessel. And a conduit. A Kattakan that can withstand that total destruction... because a Ba'Suon could not.

We don't know that he could withstand it. He can't withstand Raka doing...

You said you could help him, Railé. If he told you his true name?

No, Suonkang.

Janan, we must know. If it can save those people. If it can save the land.

I don't trust this kid or anything of Mazemoor.

It's not your decision. Gherijtana?

Yes, if he would tell me directly, I believe I can separate Raka from—

He touches Lilley's hand. Even in this no-place, it feels cold. So he grips it with both of his—the left hand that doesn't exist in the other world. They have both lost some ability to touch fully, except in this place.

"I won't leave you. And they won't take you away."

HE STANDS APART from the enastramyth's fire. Across from the flames are the Ba'Suon, his brothers and sister. They look at him with a kind of stunned caution. Night suspends them in the diffused glow of the fire. The great shadow of the diamondback fallen over him stains the dark to its deepest hue.

"Lilley?" says Janan.

He looks down to his left. The stump of his wrist wrapped in leather and the subtle, persistent pain of it, like the wound never healed. This body feels smaller in the tight confines of a breathing life. Perhaps because everything outside of it is so vast.

"Lilleysha," says Méka.

The Gherijtana says, "It's not him."

Janan takes a step to round the fire. As he looks up, the king suon bends his neck down and growls from deep in his throat. Swiftly, like a thought, the golden queen alights behind her rider and flares back her wings. The silver-gray suon bellows a warning to the stars from overhead and the southern red calls back. The king bids them no attention, only stares at the Ba'Suon on this high rock. The Suonkang extends her arm in front of Janan's chest to stop his advance.

He's loved this man for years, and he's hated him for nearly as long. In this body he feels how they're almost the same thing, like the cold from the water and the cold from the air. Different elements but they make his whole world ice. The purity of Janan's love for this body and the elements within it, the whole man encompassed in it, and the scorch of his own desire—a different kind of purity. This body, this man, is *his* harwan too. Seated in its limbs and its spine, he is no longer alone and waiting.

"Do you remember," he says to Suonkang ele Méka, "when in the gathering of this diamondback, I moved you from the flight to the catch cave?"

Her voice is strained, her gaze unwavering on his face. "Yes."

The king suon lowers his wing and extends his foreleg.

"No," Janan says. "No."

"You may follow me if you can, but it might be better if you return to Mazemoor and tell them to prepare for war. The Kattakans may yet persist in this land."

"You would let Mazemoor take the blame for your actions?" The Suonkang steps forward, her arm cutting the air. "Raka!"

He climbs onto the king's back and looks down at the other Ba'Suon. "One is very like the other."

A Covenant of Ice

"Lilley!" cries the enastramyth. "Lilley, *give me your true name.*"

The golden suon with her one eye bellows with such force it throttles the night sky. Sephihalé ele Janan shouts, *"Leave him now, Abhvihin ele Raka."* And there is a moment where the pull in his chest seems to extend beyond his spine and out toward the long waters, a thread binding him to the natural elements of this world. But it's only a discomfort. He flexes his shoulders and the king suon throws his head back, his wings flared wide, and shoves off the top of this island. The wind whips through them and they plummet to the roiling crash of the waves below.

In the wake of the ashes that had once been his family, his scream tore the cosmos apart. All the generations of time and the land in vast ranges across the expanse of his being split from end to end. His rampant knowing echoed in the cries of the ice suon that launched from the glaciers and roared beneath the sky until the canopy of the world became a flicker of crystal and burning white. Until the air bloated with the beating of wings and the keening song through near infinite petals of scales. A hurricane.

we and little brother and blood

They would follow him, a child of the void. Of chaos. His consuming of all light and life. They would take his pain and turn it into a fist so tightly meshed he could punch his way through the bowels of the earth.

But he could hurt them too. The last of his true kind.

Already his absence was a solid thing. It threw a veil over his Ba'Suon senses. He could do nothing else but tear himself from the wailing cave that he'd made of his world.

So when his screams stopped and his eyes opened, he looked upon a green land, absent of his ancestors and their ice suon.

Void of all he'd loved and destroyed.

This was a land of war, an empire called Kattaka, an army of the dead that trampled living nature in its wake. It was where he belonged.

THOUGH THE KING suon could likely fight a single whaler and two corsairs, even with their cannons and guns, he won't risk the creature. The heavy thud of the suon's heart reverberates up his legs and thighs as he sits along the diamond-patterned back, holding with his one hand the braided rope of the halter. This perfect being knows, had known for over a year, the inevitability and the rightness of this. He leans forward until the wind of their flight skates back along his shoulders and down his spine. Wind runs through his hair like fingers. He presses his lips to the smooth cold scales of the suon's armor and shuts his eyes.

Constellations pull apart in his mind.

He opens his eyes and he's standing on the deck of the Kattakan ship. The pungent smell of sumara carcass quickly soaks his senses, even sinking through his eyes so they burn. The crew are gathered in a half circle before him, their eyes wide and white, like he's a

A Covenant of Ice

ghost in their midst. They're frozen in bloody tableau with their implements of carving and harvesting in their hands. The ship creaks under the weight of the scrutiny and horror. That he appeared before them out of nothing, or so they think.

He looks at the carcass of the sumara, its smooth skin flayed back, its rib bones like curved fingers grasping for life. In the next instant it bursts into ash. The whole body, the stagnant blood, the wet sightless eyes and open jaws with its fangs already pried out for a prize. His cousin sumara now dancing matter too small to even swallow. The spinning dust of the dead creature pastes to his skin. Spitting spray from the arctic waters peppers his cheeks but can't wipe away any of the ash. He absorbs the sumara's sorrow.

He walks through the crew and the cold to the deck below. He finds Lord Shearoji in a cabin of oak and brass, a clock ticking like an incantation, nailed to the wall.

"What are you doing here? How did you get here?"

Lord General Shearoji, once such a formidable figure on the battlefields, sits now at a narrow desk with the same white eyes of his crew. He's seen the same revenant. He doesn't know what he sees.

Raka takes a seat on the narrow bed. The blankets smell of salt and an old aroma of burned dragon fat.

"Lilley," says the general, with trepidation.

"Not Lilley. You said Raka was dead. Here I am, Lord General."

Shock winds its way around the cabin like smoke. Slowly the Kattakan lord moves his hand to the pistol on his desk.

"No," Raka says. The lord stops his hand. Breathing suspends in the bowels of this ship. "Do you remember Fortune City?"

"Yes."

"You'll remember Diam the same way if you continue your journey north."

The clock converses with itself in the silence. It winnows time.

"I can't turn back," Shearoji says. "The High Lord demands I bring her an ice dragon of the deep glaciers."

"When you return emptyhanded, you can tell her if you had done as she ordered, you would have brought death with it." He looks at the gun still sitting on the desk. "I feel some compassion, so I'm choosing to warn you."

The old general just shakes his head like it's the only action left to him. "Lilley—"

"Raka."

"But how is this possible? What've you done?"

"You wouldn't understand. Your people die and bury each other in the dirt. There's nowhere for your knowing to go but into the blind depths. You don't return to the cosmos." They watch each other. Confusion and deep anger steeps in his old superior. These are the engines that drive such hollow people. But instead of looking inward to their natures, they march from their home with weapons. They make

A Covenant of Ice

weapons out of other living creatures. He says, "I killed for you."

"It was war. And you came to *me*."

"This time it isn't for you."

"What have you done with Lilley that you're commanding his body? What is this Bastard magic?"

He stands. He crosses the small cabin and thrusts his palm against the lord's forehead. Shearoji sits pinned to the desk, to the motion of the black ship of Kattaka. To the decaying aspects of this conqueror's world that his people consider indomitable.

But nothing is beyond the witness of the stars. He digs his fingers into the general's warm skin. Feels it begin to grow cold beneath his grip. The lord general trembles, the whites of his eyes crawl with bloodshot and his mouth works silently like a gasping fish flung onto dry shore. Raka tells him, "All of your people are beneath my hand."

He releases the man before the body disintegrates. The wild eyes of the Kattakan gaze on him as on a thing of terrible wonder.

SOMEHOW THEY FOUND themselves on the white sand beach in the south, in their dream Sirra Kusa. Lilley watched Janan from the tree line, standing beneath the broad leaves and arching trunks that bent nearly to the pale blue water. A hundred yards off-shore, Tourmaline splashed in glee amongst the waves, occasionally tossing happy chuffs to the bright sky.

Her golden armor captured the sun and blinded him to look upon it. It was everything they wanted, but the thread of peace in the scene was marred by a blood groove of anxiety, and pain ran from the horizon to the coast.

In a thought he was sitting beside Janan. He still wore his winter gear but he didn't feel the heat, just as he hadn't felt any cold when he sat with Raka in the tundra. In this dream, too, he had both his hands and with his restored left he reached for Janan's right and crushed it in his grip.

His harwan was also untouched by the war. His skin showed a richer tan than when they'd first met, as if he'd truly spent time in this tropical climate. His dark hair fell long and loose around his shoulders. It held a shine of deep amber in the waves. He wore a white linen shirt embroidered with gold thread in the shape of dragon scales. Lilley met his eyes with a smile. It was good to see him in such full beauty.

"Where are you?" Janan squeezed his hand with the same intensity. "Are you dead? Is that why you're able to meet me here when you never could before?"

"Na. I think… I think I'm here cause Raka's with me."

"With you?"

"Walkin around in my body. I can feel him but… not."

A warm breeze cascaded over the beach and stirred the leaves and the loose top layer of sand, but neither of them felt it against their skin. Nothing of Janan's

A Covenant of Ice

expression changed and the longer Lilley looked, the dimmer the light became. Until they were no longer sitting on the sandy shore, but instead there was snow beneath their feet and they stood facing a frozen bay, its pack ice covered in recent layers of fine white grains. The wind howled but he didn't feel it any more than he had at the beach. They still held hands.

"I dunno if I'm comin back."

Janan pressed the palm of his hand to his lips. He could feel that at least; this vision wasn't all a thin imagining. "Don't say that. Are you here? Is he here in the north?"

"I think so. But he was on the Kattakan ship."

"Shearoji's?"

"I think so."

"Then stay. Wait for us right here. Railé went after you. Méka and I are contending with the diamondback."

"Contending?"

"Raka... he doesn't want us to follow. But the enastramyth did something to protect himself and his red suon from the king suon's knowing."

"I can't control if I stay or go, Janan. It might be too late for the lad's help."

"Then try to find him in your dream."

All at once Janan grasped him, arms locked around his ribs. It could've been real for the ache and relief that flooded his limbs. But maybe this was just a memory too, conjured from the hundreds of times they'd held each other with such ferocity there seemed no separation between them. For a long time, this was the case. Even when they'd been forcibly apart, nothing of their bond had waned. His harwan.

"I reckon I've loved you my whole life, Janan. Even when I was nothin but dust to the stars. I reckon we remember through generations too, like the dragons. Not in the same way, but... in some way."

"Stop talking like you're dead."

The sun in this land was setting, from a watercolor blue to ashen dusk. "I'm cold, Janan."

"*Fight him,* Lill. We've got one more war. *Fucking fight him.* I'm coming to you."

He wanted to stay. He shut his eyes so it didn't matter if night fell. He buried his face in Janan's neck and breathed every last detail of the man.

He breathed until, opening his eyes, he was standing on the shore of the frozen bay. This time the cold bit him in half. The cold latched to his bones and his limbs and he possessed no control over a single part of himself at all.

HE OPENS HIS eyes to face the white tundra and this time it isn't memory, it is home. Tangible and true. Behind him the half-frozen bay moves with slow collisions of drift ice newly formed. As a child he used to wait with anticipation for the floes to come together enough that he and his siblings could skip across the dark waters in a game of laughing pursuit. Now he begins to walk inland toward the glacier fields. The cold nips at his cheeks like

A Covenant of Ice

playful dogs and the packed snow scuffs around the fur of his boots. He tugs the coat's hood up and around his face as ice crystals are already beginning to form on the halo of wolf fur from the moisture he's brought with him from his brief occupation of the warmer Kattakan ship. Blue dawn yawns along the jagged horizon and remains of that hue. Above him, the stars run like sandcrabs across the sky.

His legs burn but he doesn't stop walking. Now he can truly feel the unfamiliar shape of this body, its pumping blood, its subtle aches from wounds that haven't fully healed. The absence of his left hand is like a thought he can't quite articulate, so it sits unsaid in the world. More than once he wanted to somehow inhabit this man, if for no other reason than it would mean he no longer had to drag his own body from place to place and day to day. The connection to himself and the intricate workings of these biological systems were long severed. When he met Lilley, he was nothing but animated limbs and approximations of emotion. He would cut his hand in some menial task and watch with detachment as the blood collected in the wound and dripped down his skin. This was all it was, this life. A corpus of materials formed by some mechanism of nature that would eventually reclaim its creation and scatter it to the cosmos.

Yet it can love, this degradation of matter. That is the betrayal. He can obliterate all the world, but love eludes him. Power is kept apart from kindness. How is nature neutral in that outcome? How does that balance the world?

In the distance, the ice suon roar.

They know the last of the family Abhvihin has come home.

Karin Lowachee

*   *   *

THE CROWN MEETS him at the towering base of the glacier his family had called the Tusk. Its sharp longitudinal edges reminded the ancient Abhvihin of walrus canines, the deep folds in the ice like the animal's rough hide. He waits as the first five suon descend from their height and alight around him. He stands motionless as they pace, long thick muzzles dipping to sniff and nudge him. The black skin of their wings, their black tongues, fan out to capture and taste the air that he brings with him on his clothes. Even in the dim light of a northern autumn, the crystalline shards of their scales glitter with every movement, a collection of diamonds that whistle music through their hollows as the wind gusts. They're larger than the diamondback, their eyes a burning blue, and nothing but cold curls from their mouths and nostrils as they chuff in conversation amongst themselves.

He turns to the king as the creature slowly whips its tail and peels back its lips to reveal the fangs in an assertion of dominance. The king is missing patches of his paneling along his haunches, likely from a bout with a competing male, which exposes the rough black skin where the scales were torn out.

i and family and i

They remember. His breath curls in a fog and he holds out his hand.

The king tosses back his head and roars. His crown answers back, a fugue of declaration. The king extends his foreleg and Raka climbs up the bridge of crystal armor

A Covenant of Ice

and seats himself behind the suon's shoulders. The great body curves as the king positions himself to launch. The banner of his wings extend to their limit then fold along his ribs as, in one violent shove, they arrow to the sky. Then the wings fling out and beat with the volume of a million hearts.

The crown follows in their wake. They circle over the wintering tundra and more of the ice suon collect in a streak beneath them until the world becomes nothing but thunder and scream.

THEY MEET THE Kattakan ship and its armed escort of corsairs just beyond the bay. The sound of the crown's approach must have alerted the vessels. The ice suon aren't avoidant of conflict like many of their southern cousins. They don't need to be pushed to retaliate against an incursion. Here in the land of the white bears and the toothed orcas, they dart into a formation of attack.

White caps curl and spill along the hulls of all three vessels. There is no hoisted flag of truce or bellow of welcome. The ships angle out of a straight line to minimize the damage of a strafing of suon fire. Their cannons haul skyward and begin to pump fireballs toward the crown in successive lines. The air explodes with concussive booms and the crown disperses like a chandelier shot by pistol fire. Deck gunners on mounted platforms spit bullets in half-circles, following the fling of suon in their attempt to avoid the artillery. A handful of the adolescent suon catch the killing blows and tumble to the long waters. Wings

112

torn. Bellies riddled. They still try to turn back to the shore of the bay. The king screams.

He flattens his chest against the center of the king's broad back, hand locked around the armored protrusion of shoulder bone as the suon dives beneath the arc of the incoming projectiles. Raka glances behind them, beyond the whip of tail. Three queens follow in their wake, their eyes diamond blue. They caw at him in recognition. All four suon blast cold flame down upon the corsairs and freeze them bow to stern. More of the crown soar in behind and double the damage along the masts and the colonnade of cannons now in permanent flare at the clouds. The black iron now coated over with opaque ice and every individual on deck a menagerie of macabre statuary. The two ships grind to a halt, the waves against their hulls suspended in ice. The wind of the crown's passing fells some of the bodies and one of the masts. They crack open in pieces on the equally frozen deck.

A surge of exhilaration pumps through him. The sky seems to suck down his throat, he and the suon one unified breath and each exhale brings down the world.

Only the whaling ship remains. It tries to turn away from the bay, to return south.

A red streak cuts through the strike of crystal white suon. None of the crown even swing their attention to the Gherijtana boy riding the bloodred. A bulge of some sort of blinding power pushes out toward him. Raka shouts to the heedless king as the wings of the red flare back and the long tail arcs to propel the smaller body haunch-first into the flank of the king. Talons latch and the two suon

A Covenant of Ice

hurl back through the sky and down toward the cold waves below.

He's thrown from the back of the ice suon. The gray sky and spinning earth lock together in tumult. The long waters collapse in over his head, fill his mouth, and blind his eyes.

THE CAMP'S MATAS were empty. He sat alone before the central fire, staring at the leaping flames. The entire camp was quiet, the people gone, even the sky overhead was a sheet of black, starless. He could barely breathe. Maybe the fire was sucking the air from his lungs.

Gherijtana ele Railé sat down beside him. Lilley looked over.

"You found me."

The boy touched his arm. They were both clad in the same clothes of the first morning they'd met, but in this dream he still had his left hand, as in the ones with Raka. The fingers flexed as if seeking something to hold. "I've got you, Lilley. But you must tell me your true name. Let me free you from him once and for all. This is why I came here."

"I reckon it don't matter anymore."

"What doesn't?"

"If you hear my name from my lips. I don't reckon I'll survive his absence." His eyes flooded and he couldn't control it. "So much carnage."

"I know. But Janan and Méka and their suon are waiting for you. I won't let you die."

114

He looked down at both of his hands. For a minute he rubbed the palm of his left with the thumb of his right. Traced the longest lines in their bisecting of his skin. He remembered his father's hands on his shoulders. As a child he'd noticed the deep creases in those palms, both scars and the skin of identity. Hands that held tools for garden work, and *were* tools for their masters. His father had told him to never come back. To run as far away as possible into the arms of war. He had kept that promise. He'd laid down with his first lover in the bowels of death. "There ain't no real recovery, is there?"

The lad squeezed his arm. "Not entirely. But there can be healing."

He met the eyes of the enastramyth. The golden irises like a physical manifestation of this strange spirit. "My name's Havinger Lilley."

The silence wrought tight between them. The lad said, softly, "That's your born name, but it's not your true name."

"Then what is it?"

"Where do you belong, Lilley? When you reach out to nature and all of the cosmos, and it reaches back, how does it recognize you?" The Gherijtana paused. "You somehow understand the silent names of the suon. You know yours too."

All of the cosmos. He touched the harwa on his right wrist. The cool smoothness of dragonbone and sea pearl. Even in dream he felt the bond to Janan captured in the cuff. Tears choked his throat but he

A Covenant of Ice

looked the enastramyth in the eyes once more. He'd only ever given his name to one other person. Maybe this had been his harwan's fear all along. That by giving it away, he would be losing something of himself.

But maybe this boy was right. Maybe there could be healing.

"Sephihalé ele Lilley. My name is Sephihalé ele Lilley."

WHEN THE WORLD began to warm, he was curled naked before a fire with a wolf pelt cast over his body. His body remembered the tearing out and nothing of the falling down. The first time he awoke like this, under bear fur in the mata of the family Lapliang, his body remembered the falling down and nothing of the invasion. On either side of both awakening and passing out, he was gouged by death.

But his body grew warm and he was tired. Not the fatigue of sleeplessness, but the exhaustion of being welcomed, finally, into rest.

SHADOWS GREETED HIM when he opened his eyes fully. They danced at the corners of his vision, mimicking the flames. A cold wind coursed through his hair. The scent of fur and cured skin and smoke draped across his nose, the lower half of his face. Someone had erected a tent over him and staked its corners into the frozen tundra. It took some of the brunt of the wind.

Outside the tent, providing a partial bulwark against

the cold, sat Gherijtana ele Railé. Lilley stared at the edge of his shoulder and the thick coat of sealskin draped there. He said the kid's name and tried to push himself to sit without dislodging the fur from around his naked body. It remembered, suddenly, falling into the icy waters.

The enastramyth turned to look at him. "Don't move too much. You nearly drowned. I had to clear your lungs and get you warm again."

The boy had Raka's eyes.

THE ENASTRAMYTH'S STICK magic gave them their fire, and it had also pulled Raka from his body, from his being. He remembered none of it and couldn't feel anymore what Raka did. Raka was nowhere and the emptiness of it seemed to bend his ribcage back and expose his heart to this winter clime. The wind wailed through his body like his body was a cave. He wanted to mourn. He thought he'd cried somehow, that his cheeks should have been a sheen of frozen tears. It felt like he had something to grieve, like his chaos all these months had been a part of his family. His hand was missing once more.

"How will you survive him?" he asked this boy with his comrade's eyes. Raka who had become, in some twisted way, his harwan too.

The Gherijtana's inherent distracted state was twofold now. But there was no scent of smoke about him, nothing of ritual. Only the disconnected slowness

A Covenant of Ice

of his speech, his contemplations. "I'll learn. I feel him. Maybe we'll have conversations like you did, eventually. When he stops fighting. Maybe I'll resolve the pattern that'll release him back to the cosmos where he belongs. Then you'll see him again in time."

The strain had already begun in that young face. Lilley wondered if this was what Janan had seen in him. Probably more. A Ba'Suon sensed such things beyond mere sight. The smallest changes in a disrupted nature.

"So you knew you were gonna do this all along?"

He had to repeat the question.

"I knew I had to. In my dream I met you, and Raka came to me. Sometimes, though, I didn't meet you and the ice suon flew to the southern island of Kattaka and laid waste to it."

"Where're they now? Cause they ain't here. Even I can't hear em."

The Gherijtana frowned. He looked across the wind lines of the tundra for some minutes. Then he turned back to Lilley. "Take Rascal. Go south. Janan and Méka said they'd try to meet us here, but they were fighting with the diamondback. If they're not here now something must have happened. I'll stay here for now and…"

"Where's Rascal?" And when the lad didn't answer, Lilley touched his arm. Squeezed it with urgency. "Railé. Son, I reckon you need to call your dragon. Call him now."

* * *

HE RODE THE red dragon south in a kind of fugue. They left behind the boy and the frozen Kattakan ships that would eventually sink beneath the waves to join the other invaders who'd dared these waters and the dragons of the north. The dead in their fathoms of coffins, a land of night and bone. He thought of Raka the entire way, how a man born from such terrain and isolation would carry this edgeless dark even into some silhouette of love. And how he felt the absence still, like he himself had lost his shadow and walked companionless under the sun.

He and Rascal rested on the islands of the Widow's Tears when Rascal was fatigued, and he slept in the ring of the dragon's tail with the creature's breath ghosting over him to keep him warm. He didn't know what he'd done to earn the dragon's affection, or whether it was some directive compelled by Railé. Something told him the lad wouldn't do such a thing. Instead, a veil of protection draped around them, or so the enastramyth said. To keep off the cold and the eyes of those who would do them harm.

All but one of the three nights were spent in blessed oblivion. In the last night before they'd make it to Diam, he sat up under the blanket of the night sky and watched mesmerized as sheets of glowing green and sapphire blue breathed across the canopy. The waving banners of light spread from horizon to horizon and seemed to rise to the height of the stars. He stretched out his hand as if he'd be able to stroke along the silk curtain of them, and maybe the cosmos felt his intent,

A Covenant of Ice

for the light rippled as he moved his fingers across it. He breathed fully for what could've been the first time in years. The air tasted of alpine green and salt sea.

In his dream on that last night, the diamondback came to him. Raka in dragon form, soaring overhead so all he saw as he lay on his back on the dream field was the massive beast's white belly blending with the sky. Raka roared and it shook the entire earth. The ground quaked beneath him. Raka roared and a hundred ice suon answered back.

They flew in the diamondback's wake, the king of the arctic crown with his armor of crystal scales and black wings at the point of the chevron. But it was Raka, the king of the Crown Mountains, that led them. A thunderous invasion that blotted all sun, all moon, and the living light of both through the cycle of hours. Lilley watched in rising horror as they breathed their cold fire across every Kattakan settlement on the land. He remained on his back, but somehow, in this dream, he witnessed the systematic attack up and down the coastal towns, the inland villages, the mining operations and logging settlements all the way to Fortune City, which still stood in the broken and ashen remains of itself. The destruction carried from night to day and back to night again, as though in the passing of dreaded time there would be a bloody rewinding. He saw the crown from the far north finally swarm the capital city of Diam on the southern coast, where once he'd stood before the High Lord with Méka and listened to the diamondback king threaten the city for their freedom.

Now there existed no threat, only retribution. And the screams of the population cut short, abruptly, as the ice from the suon of the deep glaciers swiftly trapped them all, every person, every child, in its frozen, suffocating grip.

He sat up in his dream, heart pounding in his ears, and Raka the man came to him. He couldn't discern whether this was truly Raka or some memory of him, a way to look him in the eyes once more. To touch.

They sat on that cliffside in Kattaka, like they had once after battle long ago, except he didn't have the taste of blood in his mouth, only the memory of what he'd just watched play out. Strangely, like in all the other dreams of this man lately, his hand was restored to him, but this time the leather wrapping with which he bound his stump now suffocated his fist. As if he could no longer accept the lie of Raka's visions, or the memory of when he'd been whole. He felt the cool air off the ocean and how it brushed through his hair like a nuzzling pet. They both watched the waves roll in as a pink and orange dawn slowly stripped the lowest point of the sky of its night.

He looked at Raka's profile in that light. There was gold in his eyes instead of the total black of a void. Maybe now they could speak without artifice or agenda.

"Did you tell that diamondback to lead the northern ones to attack?"

Raka didn't look at him. "No. But maybe he knew my intent all along. Or maybe they decided on their

A Covenant of Ice

own. The ice suon have never permitted outsiders to touch their shores."

"But they left their shores."

Raka turned to him slowly. His eyes shone but not from tears. From strain. It was as if he'd been gazing too long into a scene beyond his ken. Perhaps into an abyss. "The suon have the right to protect their land. Nature will always rebalance itself."

"This is what the Greatmothers saw."

Raka didn't answer him. Maybe it no longer mattered, the visions of a future already passed. "Méka once told me I should tell you that I love you."

The shell of an egg seemed to crack in his throat. "You don't need to say it."

"Because you don't care?"

"Cause I know already. Even if the love you gave me was a killin fire."

Raka didn't dispute it. In quickened life, they would have argued about it. But maybe that was part of the fire too, one of the only things that managed to warm this man who was born in the depths of winter. He didn't know. Despite the hollow of what no longer occupied his body, maybe he'd never know. But he'd witnessed the core of this man's pain and he could no less look away any more than Raka could from the chaos he'd become. In the center of his own stunted knowing, he, too, carried a chaos long before Raka had ever walked into that camp so many years ago. To watch his mother die. To stand beneath the hands of his father, now dead. To breathe the fog of his early life and realize it was smoke, black smoke stuffing its fingers behind his tongue until it rendered him speechless. There the pain thrived, unspoken.

"You belong with him," Raka said now. The source of yet another anguish.

"I know I do." But Lilley touched Raka's hand. "And you belong with your family. If that enastramyth shows you the path, you oughtta return to em."

He didn't expect the beginning of the man's breakdown, but perhaps he shouldn't have been surprised. They had come to a standstill on this rock of their memory, where nothing of the past could be recovered, but where also nothing of the now could be destroyed.

So he wrapped his arms around Abhvihin ele Raka and clenched his hand into the Ba'Suon man's back, and so held him as he wept. After some time, he felt Raka's hands sink into his ribs. They held on together, and maybe for Raka it wasn't the same as occupying the common space of his body, but Lilley reckoned it was better.

"They'll forgive you," he said. "They'll forgive you, Raka, because I have."

The next time he opened his eyes, the sun was full against a blue, cloudless sky and he felt the yearning tug of his harwan, Janan, and their golden queen dragon Tourmaline. They were calling him home.

IT WAS AUTUMN in the southern region of Eastern Kattaka, but as he and Rascal winged over the land on

A Covenant of Ice

approach to Diam, then over the great Kattakan city itself, all he saw was ice. All of the homes, the villas like the one in which he'd been enslaved, the shops with their awnings and lanterns, the piers and fish markets that surrounded the base of the vaulting hill of the central city were all crystallized in the dragons' cold fire, the people who had been on the open streets now in frozen animation of their fleeing. Some seemed not to have even had opportunity to run, but were caught mid-gesture in poses of domestic or mundane action. Sitting on a park bench, strolling through a shopping alley, crouched in a garden. The dead in perfect diorama. Winter would overtake this land soon, perhaps before these poor souls and their world could even thaw. Surely come spring and summer the devastation would fully sink into the earth and drift in the air. The eastern island kingdom of Kattaka, once the land of Ishia as the Ba'Suon knew it, had become an open graveyard. Maybe the Ba'Suon and their dragons would burn it all before the rot set in. A cleansing fire so nature would be allowed to renew.

He almost heard Méka's voice in his mind. Two words of lamenting. *It's so*.

He found his harwan and Méka and their dragons on one of the untouched fields some miles from Diam. The specter of the city with its foreign tiled architecture and layered colorful towers still loomed in the distance, the encompassing ice shell glittering under the cool sun. From this vantage it was deceptively beautiful. A fantastical new world. A mask for slaughter.

As soon as Rascal landed, Lilley slid down his back and crossed the small patch of grass to collide into Janan's arms. Relief poured into him and he gave it back; he'd reached his oasis. But with it also the grief. That, too, sank through his skin and muscle to engrave on his bones. To feel so much sorrow trembling in this mutual grip, neither of them attempted to hold it back.

"We couldn't stop it," Janan said into his shoulder.

"I know." Both their voices as thin as bird-bone. "I saw it. I think Raka showed me." The dragon or the man, it made no difference. "Don't be angry at me. I gave the kid my name."

Janan's arms squeezed his ribs to creaking. Forestalled any more words. "I'm not angry."

Méka joined them. The three of them for some time in a silent circle of holding on. And their suon—golden, gray, bloodred—motionless and calm, their faces toward the north.

AT NIGHT THE heaviness of the new shape of their world seemed to deepen. On the one hand, no more Kattakans. On the other, so much death. What of the land? What of the empire across the long waters? What of Mazemoor?

They didn't know, but Lilley answered at least some of the questions. They built a large fire and ate from what food stores still remained from the beginning of their expedition. He couldn't recall the last time he'd eaten anything substantial besides what small game he

A Covenant of Ice

caught on his flight south with Rascal. They all sat close together, Janan and Méka on either side of him, and shared dried meat and spoke quietly. The dragons had flown for their nocturnal hunt. They heard no dragons at all.

"Where'd the diamondback go?" he said.

"We don't know," said Méka. "After…" She paused. "After, he left with the ice suon. North. Maybe back to the Crown Mountains."

"Where he belongs," Lilley said.

"It's so."

"And the ice suon?"

"Hopefully back to their land," said Janan. "Railé?"

"He said he'd call his Mazoön contacts through his…" Lilley waved his hand. "Mythicism relay. So they can go get em. I dunno though… he took…"

"Raka?" Méka said. Her voice was even more hushed, as if mentioning the name might conjure the man anew.

Lilley nodded. Their last moments in that dream, on the cliffside. He brushed his sleeve over his eyes. Janan draped an arm around his shoulders and he shook his head, though he didn't know what exactly he was denying. The weight felt good. The warmth. And it unlocked the last bolt keeping his control tightly shut.

"He took Raka into himself. I reckon he thinks he can manage it through his magic. He said that was the whole reason he came south. To find me and finish this. What Raka had started when he'd killed his family. And now there ain't nobody to track the

Ba'Suon on this island. Shearoji's ship survived but the other two're like... like here. If the general comes back to these shores he'd be a fool. I reckon he'll take the story back to mainland Kattaka. And I got the feelin if anyone else comes to this country, that diamondback'll bring his crown down from the mountains and follow up on what his northern cousins've done. What he helped em to do. I reckon Raka freed this land after all and what am I supposed to do with that? I was a part of it. It don't matter I never agreed, I was a part. So what do any of us do with that when there's alla this now around us?" The death. The lingering of death that nobody knew better than the Ba'Suon, how in the inevitable cycle of nature war shouldn't have played a part. It was an unnatural harbinger to the living world.

Méka reached over and gripped his hand. Something passed between her and Janan and Janan laid his hand upon hers. Upon them both. She said to them, "After we'd gathered the king suon on the Crown Mountains, Raka reminded me that this land has been steeped in blood for a long time. The earth is soaked in it. The stars have been witness to it for generations. Maybe this—all of this—is as the stars deem it." She gestured up to the dark heavens in the manner of the Ba'Suon. "As we all are. Even Raka. Nothing of him was against nature since he was born of it, same as you and me."

Maybe those words were true, but he knew even Méka, in her unshakable Ba'Suon knowing, would be unable to shake so much devastation. As Ba'Suon, both she and his harwan would carry the weight of

A Covenant of Ice

these deaths forward to future generations in the very air they breathed. In the turn of day to night. Carnage had become their country, and his as well. It had been so for a long time.

They huddled together in the thrown light of the fire, blankets around their shoulders. Eventually they tried to sleep. He curled against Janan's side and Méka made herself a shield at his back. Their energetic life shared as much as the warmth from the flames, and in that certainty—this quiet rebellion against all the ruin in their world—they persisted in rest.

COME SPRING, MANY of the Ba'Suon in Mazemoor began to venture back to their island in Ishia, refugees of past decades now returning to the land of their ancestors. By Phinia Dellerm'el's word, the Mazoön government was only too happy to encourage this exodus back to their homeland. Apparently, said the agent, the prospect of the northern dragons doing to Mazemoor what they had done to Eastern Kattaka frightened them into agreeability. Yes, go, said the Mazoön. Take supplies from our cities and towns. Borrow our ships to transport you and your livestock and your belongings. We will captain them for you. Just go.

Their southern cousins had other concerns, said Janan. Apparently, the conflict between different styles of mythicism was becoming more virulent. The "work" he'd done for their government in hunting down rogue enastramyths had only vaguely curtailed the rise. But this was no longer his problem or his occupation.

They spent the winter in the lower elevations of the island and away from any former Kattakan settlements. The dragons, with their natural sensitivity, avoided the dead towns and cities, so after a manner it was occasionally possible to forget that all around them death exhausted the earth. He felt it less than his harwan, their family, the Suonkang—all the Ba'Suon that set their matas in clearings by running water and towering old trees. Janan said it had become another ringing beat in the drumming of the natural world. They would learn it over time as a part of the way the stars moved. In the breadth of the cosmos, this destruction, too, would simply slip away. There would be new growth. It wouldn't be precisely the same but that, too, was part of the cycle of existence over generations. The suon taught them that daily. Living nature was a dynamic force and the ice suon had set in motion something the Ba'Suon themselves had never dared. Never could. But what they could accept in the end as nature's rebalancing, Lilley still found difficult to reconcile.

Gherijtana ele Railé returned to Mazemoor on a Mazoön whaler. Phinia Dellerm'el sent word that he was doing well, but from the young enastramyth they heard nothing specific. Lilley felt nothing, not even a nudge, if there was indeed some threat of his name being used for nefarious purposes. So he reckoned the

A Covenant of Ice

lad had spoken true. Railé had freed him by possessing the power to do the opposite.

Sometimes, though, the remnant of Raka ghosted through him like a chill wind. On these occasions he packed some supplies and hiked out across the land on his own. At first, Janan worried (Janan would worry for some time, in general, Méka said, and Lilley understood it), but eventually over the weeks when he continued to return from each of these forays, his harwan settled into the need. Sometimes he needed it, too, and Lilley let him go. Tourmaline always went with him at least. By nightfall they always returned to each other.

The rivers were running thick with snowmelt when he made camp for a day a couple miles north from where the Suonkang had staked their matas in an evergreen valley. He fished and built a fire, gutted and cleaned and cooked the trout through. He sat facing the river and let the soft meat melt on his tongue while his fingers soaked up the juices and the heat. The sound of small animals scampering through the underbrush accompanied the music of the river flow.

He heard the dragon breathing before the crash of heavy steps through brush and deadfall broke the quiet of his solitary sojourn. The broad shadow spread over him and the width of the river before he turned around and looked up to meet the burning eyes of the diamondback king. For a minute the dragon regarded him, wings back and muzzle poised like he was listening for something in the air. His black crest rose and flattened twice and then he lumbered past Lilley and into the river. A couple slaps of his wings sent the water splashing toward the camp. Lilley stood quickly and took off his hat to wave it at the dragon.

"You're an ornery fellar, I tell ya. Come here and disturb my serenity?"

The diamondback chuffed at him then sat his haunches in the river, his tail coursing over the surface of the waves. They watched each other until Lilley retook his seat by the fire and looked up at the beast who seemed perfectly content in the simple company. He marked time passing by the descent of the sun and the dragon's propensity to shift position after every half of an hour, as if following the path of light across the land. The gold diamond pattern along his spine shone in the dying day. Lilley didn't speak and neither did the dragon. If he felt anything at all it was a recognition of presence. Tranquility settled once more on this swathe of territory and sleep whispered in his ear to succumb. The destructive nature of this king dragon remained absent for the duration, until the rising moon seemed to signal him to move on.

Without any other consideration, the dragon stretched his wings and shoved himself into the air. The force of it nearly threw the river water onto Lilley's fire. With a roar that declared himself to the falling dusk, the diamondback disappeared into the clouds, leaving behind only the echo of the wind through his hundred thousand scales.

A Covenant of Ice

Lilley continued to stare at the sky long after the beast was gone. For some reason the dragon had thought to visit him, perhaps come down from the Crown Mountains where first they'd become acquainted. He wondered if in his own way, the dragon Raka missed the man, and if that were the case then maybe, from time to time, they would meet each other as old companions. Until it was no longer needed. Until, perhaps, they were both at peace.

"Let's go south to Sirra Kusa."

In the close warmth of the mata, their limbs lay tangled and the painted pictures of forest creatures made mischief on the canvas walls beside their bed. He didn't mean the suggestion as a form of fantasy escape. Janan searched his eyes to confirm the words and slowly smiled back. Hard to think there'd been a time when he hadn't been sure he'd ever see such an expression again. It wasn't that long ago, only a season, and sometimes he felt that reality heavier than most.

"But we don't know what's truly there," said his harwan.

"We got that old man's mapbook and the explorer seemed pretty accurate in his drawings of Ishia." He let his breath out and comfort sank deeper into his bones. Slowly he was getting used to this feeling—one of ease or at least some cousin of it. Maybe he'd never feel completely in the center of it, but day by day he discovered some new shade. "We'll have Tourmaline. We can just take a peek, see if any of it's got a sandy beach with clear blue water."

Janan didn't reply. Instead, he coiled a lock of Lilley's hair around his finger, watching the red catch the golden lamplight.

"Would you wanna leave your family?" Lilley asked him.

"It wouldn't have to be forever."

"No," he said. "It wouldn't."

"We can return to the paths of my family now. Cross the Derish River in the summer months."

He reached up to cover Janan's touch with his own. "Yeah, we can."

Family like Prita. Some blood cousins. Janan's parents had died from illness in the internment camp from which Méka's family had eventually been released. The cost of living in this land bore a tall tally. He knew it as well as his harwan.

"Or we could just see what there is to see in the world," Janan continued. "And maybe there'd be a land that doesn't know war."

"Maybe."

These words had grown out of the realm of musing. Now, a gathering reality. Outside, they heard Tourmaline return from her night hunt, her shuffling steps in front of their mata and the sound of her happy grunts that meant she'd made a kill and her belly was full. Soon she'd settle somewhere close and scratch at the soft velvet of her wings, and curl her tail

A Covenant of Ice

around her haunches, and eventually lower her chin to the ground. What else did they need?

"We'll leave at the first flowers," Janan said, and drew him closer.

He didn't need to say a word, not even of agreement. Not a single part of him resisted.

AT DAWN HE crept out of the mata, wrapped in the warm quilt that still carried their scent. He wandered down to the river that bisected this valley, the northern stretch of which had been his camp just hours earlier, where the diamondback Raka had found him. Here he settled on the grassy bank and watched the early light play on the ripples, making the wavelets molten. The air tasted green but also still carried the faint rotting odor of the dragons' annihilation. Some of the Ba'Suon who had fled to Mazemoor would not return. For some of them it might take generations before they could withstand the death in this land. He understood it and he thought Janan did too. So they were leaving in search of their own country. Maybe there was wilderness still left in this world.

This time, he remembered to bring his cigarettes with him. Carefully, he lit it one-handed, holding the stick between his lips. The familiar ritual of it calmed his sometimes overactive nerves. Calmed his mind, too, which still acted up and propelled him from proper sleep. And sometimes he just liked to watch the sunrise and listen for the footsteps of his harwan come to join him from their mata. Janan would leave the door open. He'd say a gentle word to a sleepy Tourmaline, and sometimes Tourmaline would answer back with a faint rumble. Then Janan would sit beside him and they'd share the cigarette. Eventually he'd wrap his arm, and the quilt, over his harwan's shoulders and they'd remain quiet in each other's presence until it didn't feel like they were separate at all. These small motions of being where they didn't have anything but the oncoming day waiting on the horizon.

Here and now, their families would eventually stir. Méka would bring them hot tea. Sometimes she'd sit with them, sipping from her own cup, and nobody would speak. It would just be him, his harwan, and this woman who'd freed him—and the soft sun opening its eye to witness the beginning again.

ACKNOWLEDGMENTS

So MANY THANKS to everyone at Solaris for working hard to support this trilogy, in particular my wonderful editor Amy Borsuk, for her kind patience and thoughtful comments that helped make these stories so much more than they were in my mind. Thank you to Charlotte Bond, once again, for her diligent attention and care in the copyediting stage. Thank you to my agent, Tamara Kawar, and everyone on the team at DeFiore & Company. Thank you to the many readers and people in literary media across the world who have buoyed my work through the years, and who continue to rise against the threat of censorship and book banning by celebrating writers and writing. Thank you to my friends, both my fellow writers and the ones who've come up with me through the years who stand with me in love and appreciation for the written word and storytelling. It is powerful, which is why those who are afraid of truth seek to control or abolish it. In particular, to my lifetime sisters Winnie and Yukiko, who have known me and encouraged me as a writer long before I was published.

And, finally, so much of these stories are about family and I want to thank mine—who have read my work, come to my book launches, asked me about my projects or otherwise been proud and interested: Colin, Michaele, Sharon, Sean and Eve. Tony, Maureen, and John. Joanne, Hayden, Olivia and Dustin. Simone and Greg. Beloved Johann, Mrinal, Malaika and Parinidhi. Neil and Indira. Jeri, Tiffany, Lucas, Paige and Sam. Richlynd, Jo'Ann, and Deirdre. And also in loving memory: Cliff, Esther, and Ray. Joe, Catiline, and Lance. My grandfathers in particular were avid readers, and my grandmothers a teacher and a motorbike riding fashionista, respectively. Also, to my sweet Coco for inspiration for the suon, and usurping my lap and attention when I'm trying to write. Being chosen by an animal who bonds to you is truly a gift. Sometimes family is four-legged.

ABOUT THE AUTHOR

Karin Lowachee was born in South America, grew up in Canada, and worked in the Arctic. She has been a creative writing instructor, adult education teacher, and volunteer in a maximum security prison. Her novels have been translated into French, Hebrew, and Japanese, and her short stories have been published in numerous anthologies, best-of collections, and magazines. When she isn't writing, she serves at the whim of a black cat.

@karinlow.bsky.social
@klstoryteller
karinlowachee.com

FIND US ONLINE!

www.rebellionpublishing.com

/solarisbooks   /solarisbks

/solarisbooks   /solarisbooks.
bsky.social

SIGN UP TO OUR NEWSLETTER!

rebellionpublishing.com/newsletter

YOUR REVIEWS MATTER!

Enjoy this book? Got something to say?

Leave a review on Amazon, GoodReads or with your favourite bookseller and let the world know!